"My friends call me Danny."

Meg refused to budge despite his proximity; she tilted her head up and met the undisguised twinkle in his gaze. She bit back a sigh, met Danny's gaze with an equanimity she didn't feel and angled her head slightly. "But we're not friends."

He grinned. "We might be in two months. Wouldn't hurt to get in practice, Miss Russo. After all, we *are* going to be neighbors."

And that's all they'd be. She'd make certain of that. She gave him an over-the-shoulder glance as she descended the stairs. "Megan. My friends call me Meg."

Danny's grin deepened. "Can I move in tomorrow?"

She withdrew a key from her front pocket and dangled it in front of him. "Whatever works for you." She stuck out a hand once he accepted the key and flashed him a smile. "Welcome to Jamison."

Books by Ruth Logan Herne

Love Inspired

Winter's End
Waiting Out the Storm
Made to Order Family
Reunited Hearts
Small-Town Hearts

*Men of Allegany County

RUTH LOGAN HERNE

Born into poverty, Ruth puts great stock in one of her favorite Ben Franklinisms: "Having been poor is no shame. Being ashamed of it is." With God-given appreciation for the amazing opportunities abounding in our land, Ruth finds simple gifts in the everyday blessings of smudge-faced small children, bright flowers, fresh baked goods, good friends, family, puppies and higher education. She believes a good woman should never fear dirt, snakes or spiders, all of which like to infest her aged farmhouse, necessitating a good pair of tongs for extracting the snakes, a flat-bottomed shoe for the spiders and the dirt…

Simply put, she's learned that some things aren't worth fretting about! If you laugh in the face of dust and love to talk about God, men, romance, great shoes and wonderful food, feel free to contact Ruth through her website at www.ruthloganherne.com.

Small-Town Hearts

Ruth Logan Herne

Love Inspired

Recycling programs for this product may not exist in your area.

LOVE INSPIRED BOOKS

ISBN-13: 978-0-373-81556-2

SMALL-TOWN HEARTS

Remember not the sins of my youth and my rebellious ways; according to Your love remember me, for You are good, O Lord.
—*Psalm* 25:7

Dedication

To Aunt Isabelle and Gram, two stout-hearted ladies who rescued me more than once. I know God has a special place in heaven for both of you. Keep a rocker handy with my name on it… We'll rock babies together.

Acknowledgment

Big thanks to Lynn McCutcheon and Richard Buckles for their added information about the Great Wellsville Balloon Rally and hot air ballooning. To Don and Karen of the Angelica Sweet Shop, your charming establishment lures people in. The great staff and wonderful selection do the rest. To Anita Green whose dedication to her daughter Michelle is true inspiration to this author. To Dave, who drove the truck back to "Sandy's Place" on Route 19 to pick up my swing. Gulp…

To the Sekler family who first drew me to Wellsville for the Little League state championship in '07. You got the ball rolling.

Huge thanks to Mandy, who road-tripped Allegany County with me before and will again, only this time we get to bring "Mary Ruth" along. God is, indeed, good. And I'd be remiss not to acknowledge the amazing help of my children and their spouses and our good friend Paul, in many different ways. Their never-ending gifts of time, effort, money and baseball tickets have helped keep us afloat during rocky times, and that's what family's all about. God truly blessed me with each and every one of you. And do I have to name you all again? Seriously???

Chapter One

"Ben! No!"

A shriek pulled Danny Romesser's attention across the cobbled historic street nestled beneath deep-green maple arches, the early summer day a gift from God.

Right up until then.

He swung around, watching, helpless from this distance.

The young woman's admonition only intensified the unfolding drama as a young man with Down syndrome withdrew a plump, ripe mango from the base of a perfectly mounded boardwalk display. The fruit toppled, one nudging the next, the mangos and peaches free-falling their way to the broad wooden surface below.

"Oh, Ben..."

Distress laced the woman's voice while the mentally challenged young man stood nearby, clasping and unclasping his hands in typical Down fashion, his face a study of remorse, his voice loud and earnest, stirring Danny's memories. "I-I'm sorry, Meggie. I didn't touch a thing, I really didn't."

The woman stared, dismayed, a picture herself, dressed in historic garb that seemed oddly in place here in Jamison, New York.

She grimaced, set a sizable basket down, glanced at the tiny clock pinned to her chest and bent low to retrieve the fruit.

"Not again?"

An irate man with thinning hair pushed through the front door of the nineteenth-century-style mercantile, set in the middle of a Brigadoon-like village that seemed to have stopped the clock about the time Danny's great-grandma Mary was born.

Possibly before.

If the guy's scowl pumped Danny's adrenaline, his ensuing tirade literally pulled him into action.

"How many times do we have to go through this, Megan?"

"Mr. Dennehy, I—"

"Too many," the older man thundered, not giving the young woman time to reply, red splotches marking his thin face. "If he—" he pointed a bony finger at Ben, his voice rising "—doesn't have the good sense to avoid my displays, then you certainly should! There is…" his voice cooled with disdain as he switched the direction of his finger to the opposite side of the street "…another perfectly good sidewalk over there."

Memories of Uncle Jerry surged forth as Danny approached, how Danny had defended the much older man from the jeers and taunts of ill-mannered people who considered him little more than the village idiot. Kids could be heartless and cruel. Adults, too, from time to time, as evidenced by the grocer's harangue.

"I need your word, Megan."

The young woman straightened, chagrined, the last of the fruit picked up and deposited in a small grocery cart. Danny saw a flash of anger mixed with consternation. She ignored his approach and kept her gaze trained on the shopkeeper. "It won't happen again, Mr. Dennehy."

"It's happened four times." His tone didn't cut her any slack. "That's three times too many."

"I-I'm really sorry, Mr. De-henny," the young man offered.

His tone spiked feelings within Danny. But he had no idea what he could do to help. He only knew he wanted to interrupt the man's verbal smackdown of both the woman and the mentally challenged young man.

The young man noticed him. "Hey, Mister, you wanna buy some chocolate?"

The woman and the grocer turned his way, the conflict forgotten momentarily. That was good, right? Danny jumped into the fray with a nod toward Ben. "Sure. Do you sell chocolate, sir?"

The respectful title lightened the woman's features

with a flash of pleasure. She inclined her head toward Ben, her patience allowing him to continue what he started. A good trait, Danny knew, and not one easily attained.

"M-Meggie makes the best chocolate around." Ben swiped away a tiny spit bubble with the back of his sleeve. The grocer grunted disapproval. Danny nodded, patient.

"We have chocolate crunch, almond, plain and..." He hesitated, looking to Meggie for help. "I don't remember."

Her gaze softened, giving her an air of measured gentility and rare beauty, like the warmth of a fall fire on a crisp October evening. "Caramel biscotti."

That combination drew Danny's attention. She had caramel biscotti chocolate? He eyed her more closely, trying to get beyond the historic costume that made her what? Amish? Quaker? Crazy?

In New York or Boston, yes.

But here, in this quaint village of beautifully restored old buildings and a cleverly worn boardwalk, *charming* was the better word. The gold, green, red and ivory calico was too bright to be Amish and he hadn't heard a *thee* or *thou* yet.

He'd go with *delightful*.

And remarkably good-looking. Curly golden-brown hair peeked from beneath the ruffled edge of a deep green bonnet, and a dusting of matching freckles dotted fair skin along her nose and upper cheeks. Long lashes framed light brown eyes with tiny hints of amber sparking miniscule points of light. The fitted dress was nipped and tucked to form, and he couldn't help but notice it nipped and tucked in all the right places.

"I'll take one of each," he told Ben.

Ben's head bobbed in excitement. "Meggie, do you have that many in your basket?"

"I do."

Bright and carefree, her voice lilted, making him want to hear her speak again.

Danny turned. She fished in her basket and came up with four bars of cello-wrapped chocolate, the varieties marked by copper lettering. He eyed them, surprised, expecting the traditional fundraiser candy bars. These were different.

She raised her gaze to his and eyed him, probably wondering what his problem was. Either that or he read a tiny spark of awareness before she shut it down.

Interesting.

Gaze calm, she faced him, expectant, waiting.

Money.

She needed money for the chocolate. Of course. He plunged his hand into his pocket and came up totally blank. Absolutely empty. His wallet held his debit and credit cards, his license and nothing else. No cash. Since he rarely needed cash, he'd gotten out of the habit of carrying much. Embarrassed, he withdrew his debit card and shook his head. "No cash. Sorry. You don't have a credit card machine tucked in that basket, do you?"

Her look shadowed, his humor unappreciated.

Danny waved a hand, indicating the town. "Where's the nearest ATM?"

She dipped her chin and tilted her head in exaggerated but genteel puzzlement. "I know not of what you speak, sir."

He jerked his head toward the street. "An ATM. Surely there must be one in this..."

"Sweet historic village?"

A smart aleck. And impudent, at that. Her gentle air belied the quick look she sent him.

Ben turned his gaze from Danny to Meggie and back. "You don't want them, Mister?"

"I do," Danny explained, "but I have no money with me."

"If you're poor we can just give you candy, can't we, Meggie?" Ben's tone implored the woman to understand Danny's plight. Her returned look said she'd rather be giving Danny a boot in the rear for getting Ben's hopes up.

"No." Her voice firm, the young woman ignored Ben's pout of indignation and held a hand up to stave off his coming argument. "If this gentleman wants candy bars, Ben, he can come to the store with money."

"He might forget."

From Ben's disappointed expression, Danny figured a lot of people "forgot" things where he was concerned. "I won't forget." He gave Ben a look of assurance. "I promise."

Meggie's dismayed expression said she doubted his word and wished he'd left well enough alone, but Danny refused to be insulted or dissuaded. He'd find their store and buy the bars of chocolate, as promised.

Meggie's cool look of disregard said she wasn't embracing his pledge. She turned back to the grocer, deliberate. "I'll stop back to pay for the fruit after work. I'd go home for money now but I'm running late."

The grocer grunted, unappeased.

She tucked the bars back into her basket, inclined her head and offered Danny a slight curtsy, a mix of gentility and in-your-face rolled into one cute, smooth move. "My brother and I best be on our way, good man. Much to do in our sleepy little burg, you know."

She took Ben's arm and led him away, leaving Danny sputtering. He held his debit card aloft as if trying to convince someone of his worth, then realized since he was in Allegany County incognito, to find store space for a Grandma Mary's Candies tribute store, it might be smarter to stop drawing attention to himself like some madman in the street.

"Meggie, he doesn't know where the store is," Ben exclaimed, excited and alarmed. "How will he f-find us if he doesn't know where we are?"

"He makes a good point." Danny stepped forward,

a part of him wondering why her untrusting expression didn't match the spritely voice.

She leveled him a look that offered warning and resignation, then seemed to rethink her choices. Without a sound she reached into the old-world basket, withdrew a card, handed it to him and touched Ben's arm again. Ben went along this time, but he paused a store-width away, turned back and hollered, "See you later, Mister!"

"I'll be there, Ben."

Megan Russo heard the words and bit back a retort. First, the guy seemed sincere, but experience had taught her that sincerity and good-looking men were not exactly synonymous, even guys with magnetizing gray eyes, wonderfully sculpted square chins and short, dark, almost military hair. If she was judging on a "yum-factor," which she most assuredly was *not,* this guy topped the meter.

Luckily, she'd chucked her meter into the trash last fall when her former fiancé left her waiting at the church, calling off their wedding by text message.

Second, she refused to carry things any further in Ben's hearing. Once Ben's heart was set on something, nothing short of a good night's sleep could shake it loose. The simplicity of that sounded endearing, until Ben latched on to something the family didn't control and couldn't deliver. Heartbreak came easy to her younger brother.

"Ben, I'm working on fudge this morning. Would you like to help?"

"Can I ch-chop the nuts?"

"Absolutely. Save my tired arms."

He grinned, the thought of being helpful lighting the curved planes of his face, the downward tilt of excited eyes. "Thanks, Meggie."

She gave him a shoulder nudge that made him laugh. "Don't mention it, big guy. And stay away from Mr. Dennehy's tables. From now on we're walking on the opposite side of the street. Got it?"

Ben's flash of guilt confirmed what she'd suspected. He loved the sight and sound of the tumbling fruit, an impetuous five-year-old tucked in the body of a man. But naughty escapades like this weren't cute or funny. And Ben knew better.

Meg bit her lip and swallowed a sigh. Disciplining Ben was a fine line between the errant child within and the husky man beside her. But he'd made one decision quite easy for her. If they had to walk through Jamison again, she'd take him down the opposite boardwalk, along the array of shops facing Dennehy's Mercantile. He'd have a harder time wreaking havoc in front of the quilt shop, or the antique store; calico yard-lengths were not nearly as fun as tumbling fruit.

"Wh-when do you think he'll come, Meggie?"

Megan swallowed a bitter retort, scolded herself inwardly for being a crab and pushed the guy's crisp, clean image out of mind. "We'll know when he gets here, Ben." She touched Ben's arm as they rounded the corner to her two-and-a-half-story gingerbread-style house, the pink, green and ivory fairy-tale look in keeping with Meg's old-fashioned business. "Hey, looks like the finches are throwing a party in their condo." She'd deliberately put up a multilevel finch house for Ben's enjoyment. Watching the tiny birds nest successfully in the backyard of her corner lot was more beneficial than endless TV, and it kept Ben's imagination brewing.

"I love the little birds."

"I know you do." Hoping Mother Nature would help keep Ben's mind off the clock, Meg did her best to tuck the morning's events aside, including the guy's teasing glint, his questioning appraisal of her attire and a look that said he might have just landed in an alternative universe.

Welcome to Jamison.

Chapter Two

Danny read the business card she'd handed him and felt his heart downslide to somewhere in the vicinity of his gut. He sighed, a feeling of inevitable doom descending.

He turned and offered the grocer a hand along with a partial introduction, knowing that prices spiraled up when people knew he was scouting for real estate. Better to fly under the radar at this point. "Danny Graham. Pleased to meet you."

"John Dennehy. Likewise." The irritated man shrugged one shoulder west as Meggie and Ben proceeded down the tree-lined street. "They need to keep better control of Ben these days. He's not a little kid anymore."

"Accidents happen. Is there a hotel or motel nearby?" Danny refused to get into a discussion of how the mentally challenged should be kept on a short leash. He understood their limitations better than most, and knew that community involvement was in everybody's best interests.

"In Wellsville." The grocer jutted his chin south. "And there's the B and B up the road. Nice place."

Danny had noted the classic colonial bed-and-breakfast on the way in, but he was looking for something more long-term. He shook his head. "Wellsville, huh?"

John Dennehy nodded. "Closest thing, 'cept for the campgrounds on the other side of Baldwin's Crossing."

He'd seen the campground sign as well, but that wouldn't do, either. He shrugged. "Wellsville it is. I'm surprised with how pretty your village is that no one's built anything closer to service the seasonal tourists." Wellsville was a good fifteen minutes south of Jamison.

"Oh, they've tried, especially with the interstate so close," John admitted, his lips thinned. "There's development, then there's development, if you know what I mean. These days it's best knowing just what kind of life you're after before sayin' yes to every character that barrels through, wantin' to build somethin'."

The store owner's manner insinuated that Jamison might be an unlikely spot to approve his storefront development, but he wasn't in town looking for a fight. He was here to make his grandmother's dream come true, to open a store dedicated to her mother, his great-grandmother, the original Grandma Mary.

He gave John a direct and polite smile, determined to take his time, learn the lay of the land and not step on toes.

As John began wheeling the cart of damaged fruit inside, Danny held up a hand to stop him. "I'd like to buy this fruit."

The grocer scowled, thinking he was kidding.

Danny jerked his head toward the emblems on the mercantile door that said despite its historic appearance, the store accepted plastic in multiple forms. "And can you tell me where the nearest ATM is?"

John sized him up, shrugged and pressed his lips into a line. "You don't have to buy the fruit. I shouldn't have gotten so upset. He can't help that he's—"

Danny cut off the possible insult smoothly. "Challenged. Exactly. But I know a place that can use this fruit. Of course a discount would be in order."

John's gaze turned hopeful. He shrugged and nodded. "I can't say I wouldn't be grateful. And the coffee shop at the end of the row has an ATM. The banks in Wellsville have them as well. Or you can select Cash Back when you pay for the fruit."

Danny nodded, replanning the flow of his day to include a stop at the Colonial Candy Kitchen to make good on his promise.

The young woman had eyed him with suspicion when he'd raised Ben's hopes. How much lower would her opinion go when she realized he was heir apparent to Grandma Mary's Candies, one of the largest chocolate confectioners in the Northeast, and that his job would most likely include putting her out of business?

He bit back a sigh, put his game face on and helped John bag the fruit, contemplating this new wrinkle. Big cities like New York, Philly and Boston welcomed expansion and development. But here, in this sweet, historic village…

The phrase she used drew an inner smile as he remembered the tilt of her head, the arch of her brow.

Here he might be seeing his competition face-to-face every day, and he didn't like that. Not one little bit.

"Megan?"

Hannah Moore jogged toward Megan and Ben, her modern running gear a stark contrast to Megan's colonial costume. She glanced at her sports watch, paused for breath, then nodded toward the candy shop door. "Running late?"

"Grrr…"

Hannah's sympathy turned into an understanding

smile. "Well, the library doesn't open until three. Want some help?"

"Seriously? Yes."

The smile deepened to a grin. "I'll grab a quick shower and head back. I wondered why I didn't see your car here on my first pass through."

Hannah regularly ran the paths winding up and down the rolling countryside. Since Megan couldn't imagine running down the block, much less up a smallish mountain, she held Hannah in high esteem.

"The car's in the shop for a few days. And Ben's got today off, so…"

Hannah flashed a smile of understanding and welcome Ben's way. "So you get to hang out here today, huh, big guy?"

Ben beamed. "With Meggie."

"And me." Hannah sent Megan a look that said more than words, and headed south. "I'll be back in a little bit."

"Thanks, Hannah."

Megan watched her retreating back as Hannah wound her way beneath the trees, heading for home. For a fleeting moment she wondered what it would be like to have Hannah's athleticism and freedom, the chance to just go off and do whatever you wanted a good share of the time.

But she refused to dwell on their differences. Hadn't Reverend Hannity just offered a delightful homily equating God's timing with gardens, using metaphors like "the flowers of tomorrow are held in the seeds of yesterday" and "take the time to cultivate the garden within"?

Meg swallowed a sigh.

Right now her internal and external gardens were weed-riddled, and while she appreciated the good reverend's warmth and wit, she'd give anything to feel like she was in charge of her life, at least part of the time. But between work constraints, helping with Ben and dealing with the aftermath of her public humiliation, she pretty much felt like a puppet on a string.

"Thanks for bringing me to work with you, Meggie."

Ben's sincerity offered the kick she needed. She had much to be grateful for, starting with a business she'd built and loved, a sweet apartment upstairs that allowed independence and proximity to her store, a beautiful hometown just beginning to plow its way out of an economic backslide, and family and friends that loved her.

She refused to acknowledge what so many knew, that she'd been unceremoniously dumped by boyfriends twice in the past several years. She climbed the wide, wooden front steps of the candy store and grinned at Ben. "Glad to have you on board."

His smile tipped her world back on its axis, the sweet, impish grin a quality that couldn't be bottled. Ben might have the inquisitive nature of an errant child, but he didn't have a mean bone in his body, and there were plenty of people who could take a lesson from that.

"Hannah, that looks great." Meg indicated the neon-colored lollipops and nodded approval, the eye-catching array complementing the season. "Picture-perfect. Total attention grabber."

"Nothing to compare with what approacheth from yonder stone parking lot. Take heed!" Hannah pseudowhispered as she crossed into the production kitchen, her eyes teasing. "A man of certain breeding and gentility comes hither. Might we ready some tea for him, perchance?"

Megan shot her a withering look, glanced through the front window and decided the hop, skip and jump in her chest was a leftover sugar high from not sticking to diet soda. She dusted her hands on her apron, tucked the look of surprise away, headed for the counter and faced the door as their early visitor reappeared. He met her gaze and grinned.

Knowing how his easy demeanor had affected her defenses earlier, she should have sent Hannah to the counter. But she didn't, which meant she was either healing or a glutton for punishment.

Hannah moved forward, glancing at her watch. "Miss Russo, might I by your leave long enough to deliver today's cookies to the mercantile and café just shy of the village green?"

Megan rolled her eyes, met Hannah's gaze and

nodded at the obvious ploy. "As always, I am grateful for your help, Miss Moore."

"As am I for the gainful employment, Miss Russo."

The man swept them an appreciative look. "Obviously whatever's in the water down here is contagious. If I stay for a few weeks, will I begin to talk like that, too?"

Megan regarded him with care, a hint of amusement lifting her voice, much as it had an hour earlier. "If one were to linger and reside amongst the genteel of yesteryear, one would surely find their faith, warmth and culture most contagious, kind sir. Do you plan to take lodgings in this vicinity?"

"If that's your cagey way of asking if I plan to be in town awhile, the answer is yes. I have business here."

Hannah pushed through the front door with a wave. "I shall leave you to your verbal sparring while I deliver these forthwith."

Megan watched Hannah go with mixed feelings. Volleying words with this guy was easy with others around. Somehow it felt less natural on her own. She busied herself righting a rack of flavored candy sticks that didn't need straightening, their old-world appeal and low cost an invitation to purchase in bulk.

The man reached into his pocket and withdrew cold, hard cash, a welcome sight in a retail establishment. He eyed the credit card machine on the counter with a look of disbelief, then turned to her. "You said you couldn't take credit cards."

"And such as this is true, kind sir, two blocks from my place of business, in the middle of the street at break of day."

He frowned and moved closer to the counter, giving Megan a clear view of those gray eyes, light in the middle, their color deepening as the iris widened. His straight, dark hair stopped a hint longer than military length, and the square set of his jaw marked him as a man of decision. But in Megan's recent experience, men of decision quickly pivoted into indecision where matters of forever were concerned, so she wasn't about to believe anyone's chin, no matter how delightfully rugged it appeared.

He angled his head while waiting for her to conclude her perusal, as if accustomed to women sizing him up.

Totally understandable, considering his appearance.

She bit down a sigh, put a serene face in place and inclined her head. "But as you bear witness, kind sir, I have a machine of that nature here."

"Oh, I see all right." He let his gaze rest upon her for long seconds, his look inviting challenge. "I think I'm reading you loud and clear, Miss...?"

"Megan." She gave a slight curtsy, very much in character. "Megan Russo, in actuality, the proprietor of this establishment and sister to Benjamin, the fine young man who made your acquaintance this morning."

His smile deepened. Broadened. He held out a hand. "And I'm Daniel Graham, but my friends call me Danny."

"Whereas I am scarce an acquaintance of yours, I shall be delighted to call you Mr. Graham." She sent him a quick, smiling look over her shoulder as she moved along the counter, hoping he'd follow.

He did.

She bit back a grin, wishing this weren't fun, wishing he weren't absolutely adorable, wishing she hadn't been burned twice already and fairly certain that public humiliation was her permanent Facebook status, since that seemed to be how her life rolled these days. *Focus, Meg. Ignore the cleft in his chin, the crinkled eyes and that light of awareness. Remember, you don't know him, and probably wouldn't like him if you did.*

She paused once she had the counter between them and offered him an expectant look. "How might I be of help to you this day, good man?"

It had to be wrong to think anyone was this cute, this over-the-top, heart-stoppingly magnetic. Right?

Danny tried to prevent his reaction, to no avail. She captivated him, plain and simple. The look, the quirky nature, the spunk, the knowing smile. He hadn't reacted to a woman like this in, well…

Ever.

He'd had a variety of relationships over the years, and knew way too many Saks Fifth Avenue-friendly types from his years in Philly and New York, coupled with his regular excursions to Grandma Mary's sprawling Northeast venues.

Nothing prepared him for the total impact of this quaintly clad young woman whose eyes held challenge and maybe, just maybe, a hint of cynicism, enough to make him wonder why and how it got there in a locale saturated with small-town goodness.

He tamped the feelings down, realizing he was simply experiencing a normal, healthy reaction to a new situation because no one in big cities wore quaint, full-skirted gowns made of the sweet calicos his grandmother employed in her quilt making. And the quiet swish of the dress as Megan moved…

Just made him wish she'd move more.

He frowned inward and outward, chasing his errant thoughts away. "I've come to buy the candy bars I wanted to purchase earlier."

She nodded, slid open the door of an immaculate glass display case and withdrew a wicker basket of wrapped bars. She set the basket on the counter. Danny glanced around, noting the layout, and turned back, nodding. "You've picked a good location for the chocolate with summer here. This side of your display is shadowed enough to keep the temperature from fluctuating."

One sculpted brow arched in quiet accord. "Chocolate is a delicacy, indeed. If one does not take care to manage it with an eye toward temperature control, one can ruin a batch forthwith. And exposure to the sun will gray it, drawing the composition oils to the surface. Most unappealing."

He smiled as he withdrew eight bars. "I don't find a thing in this store unappealing, Miss Russo."

She dipped him another curtsy of acknowledgment, having no idea what her antics were doing to his heart. Or maybe she did. He withdrew another four bars just because he needed to do something that didn't include staring at her.

"Danny!"

He turned, saved by the excited lilt of Ben's voice. Ben charged forth, open and friendly, not a hint of reticence about him. Danny grinned, acknowledging the warmth, the innocence, the inborn effusive nature. He held out a hand. "I told you I'd come back, didn't I?"

"Yes." Ben turned a scolding look to his sister. "See, Meggie? I told you not to be so grumpy. I told you he'd come back. Didn't I? Huh?"

She didn't miss a beat, just turned her head, gave the young man a quick, friendly nod and smiled. "You did, Ben. I knew I should have heeded your advice."

"Yes." Ben nodded, his expression firm. "I know a lot of things, and people should listen to me more."

Megan acknowledged that with a calm look of

assent. "I would be well-advised to do so. And Ben, I see other customers approaching. Would you be so kind as to take Mr. Graham's money for his purchases?"

"I get to handle money? Yes, I'd be very glad to do it, Meggie!"

She bestowed a gentle smile of understanding on her brother, sent Danny a "gotcha" look that he didn't think existed in colonial times and moved off to take care of the new customer, the quiet whisper of her dress marking her exit.

"H-how many candy bars do you want, D-Danny?"

He laid the bars on the counter. "All of these."

Ben shot him a look of pure, unmitigated excitement, an expression that made Danny miss Uncle Jerry even more. So sweet. How he wished he'd taken more time to spend with Jerry those last years. How foolish he'd been to assume anything lasted forever.

"Twelve!"

He nodded and handed over two twenties, determined to pay in cash despite the handy machine atop the uncluttered glass counter.

He'd noticed right off that everything in the shop glowed with cleanliness. She'd gone with a white kitchen setting that embraced the store's name, the wainscoted walls, window trim, cupboards and drawers all done in a white satin finish, the old knobs a throwback to earlier times. A few small white tables graced the end of the room while the candy faced the shaded northeast side, where aged, sprawling maple trees offered a cooling, shadowed presence. The west side of the store held an ice cream parlor setup, not too big, just enough to help augment summer sales.

Smart.

Danny liked and appreciated retail intelligence. Covering the bottom line was intrinsic to business, and in her own way, Megan Russo was doing just that, filling needs to fit the season and her cash flow. And looking really good, to boot.

She picked that moment to glance their way, her look noting Ben making change, and then Danny.

Her calm gaze did a little stutter-step, just enough to make him think she felt the connection. Her quick reversion to a more reserved countenance said she had every intention of fighting it, just like him.

He almost breathed a sigh of relief, then laughed at himself. He was only here a short while, just long enough to set up a site that proclaimed Grandma Mary's cared about its roots, and while he wasn't a history buff by any means, he was smart enough to recognize how far his family had come in four generations.

Amazing.

Megan flashed another look Ben's way, and Danny's inner hopes dimmed as realization set in.

He might put her out of business. Correction: *would* most likely put her out of business.

And that meant Ben would be out of a job, a

chance to mingle with people, to feel good about himself. Danny knew how important those qualities were to the developmentally challenged.

He smiled his thanks to Ben and hoisted the bag of chocolate. "Thank you so much, young man."

Ben grinned appreciation. "You're welcome."

Danny turned and headed for the door, wishing she'd call out. Wish him good day. Say goodbye. Invite him to come again.

She didn't.

And he refused to turn, looking for her attention, knowing it was best to avoid her as much as possible considering the circumstances. The idea of causing her problems weighed on him, but his allegiance to his family business and family roots went deep. He'd scour the area for likely settings and try to place their new store far enough away from the Colonial Candy Kitchen to minimize the effect—but in the end, business was business.

Right now, he wasn't all that certain he liked that idea.

Chapter Three

"Spill it, girlfriend. Who was the hunk you were shamelessly flirting with while I delivered cookies to the mercantile and the coffee shop?" Hannah tossed out the question once the store was empty at midday.

"Some businessman."

"And then some." Hannah's arched brows and grin showed proper appreciation. "What kind of business?"

Meg shook her head, wiped down crumbs from the cookie station and crossed to the freezer. The walk-in unit had been last year's capital expenditure and was worth its weight in gold, which was almost what the unit cost. "No idea."

"You didn't ask?"

"No."

"Why?"

"Not my business."

Hannah stopped filling the half-pound boxes of

pecan caramel turtles, a big seller regardless of the season. "Meg, he told you outright he was staying around awhile."

"And?"

Hannah made a knocking motion against the counter with her left hand. "Um, hello? Opportunity calling? Sorry we missed you."

Meg sent her a scowl that was only half pretend. "Opportunity has knocked before, remember? And I answered. Big mistake. Crashed and burned. Do the words 'public spectacle' come to mind?"

Hannah's gaze softened. "You're blowing things out of proportion, Meg."

"Am I?" Meg turned, not sure that she was ready to face this conversation but not seeing an easy way out. "Are you forgetting that fiancé number one cheated on me and got another girl pregnant?"

"Which says a lot about *his* lack of character, not yours. He was totally unworthy of you and you know it."

Meg had heard that before, and had almost come to believe it when in came Michael, fiancé number two. What on Earth had she been thinking? Was she that much in love with the idea of being in love? Or just totally naive?

"Let's not forget Michael."

"No, please, *let's* forget Michael." Hannah mock-shuddered, her expression underscoring her words. "Yes, he was funny and charismatic, but he had no work ethic and little pretense of faith, and didn't Alyssa Michaels tell you he just got fired from his latest job because he failed to show up, time after time? Were you thinking you could fix that? Fix him? Not hardly."

"You're right, I know that, it's just…" Megan grimaced and shrugged. Her friend Alyssa had made it a point to call her and fill her in on Michael's newest gaffe, showcasing how undependable he was. Why hadn't she noticed that sooner? "Obviously I'm either too needy or gullible. Maybe both. Very honestly, the thought of putting myself out there again scares me to death."

"I know."

Something in Hannah's soft tone said she understood too much. A hint of sadness shadowed her eyes, her gaze, then disappeared as she moved forward to hug Meg. "But I also know that you befriended me when I moved here. I knew no one, I had no family in this area, and you reached out to me. Talked to me. You brought God's peace into my life at a time when I needed it, Meg. I want to be able to do the same for you."

Meg returned the embrace, grateful for the connection. Alyssa had been nudging her much the same way, but taking those first steps seemed harder than she'd have ever thought possible.

Hannah stepped back, eyed the clock and gave a

low whistle. "And on that very emotional note, I've got to fly if I want to get the library open by three."

Meg nodded and grabbed her hand. "Hannah. Thanks."

Hannah shrugged. "Hey, we're girls. Been there, done that. Girlfriends have to stick together. And sometimes give one another a well-meaning push."

"Which means I get to do the same for you sometime?"

Hannah waved a hand in the air as she headed for the door. "Right now we're talking about *you,* not me. See ya."

Meg grinned at her retreating back. Noting that Ben was still out back with the late-afternoon renewed antics of the finch families, she began unpacking ice cream counter supplies when the phone rang, a welcome interruption from errant happily-ever-after thoughts.

"Colonial Candy Kitchen, Meg speaking. How can I help you?"

"Meg, this is Jacqui Crosby."

Okay, make that *was* glad of the interruption. Meg was never too thrilled to chat with fiancé number one's intrusive mother. "Jacqui, how are you?"

"Frazzled and frantic, totally out of character for me, as you well know."

Meg knew no such thing. Jacqui Crosby was a town gossip, one of those people who could be counted on to spread information with hawklike speed, always watching and sharpening her tongue at others' expense. Meg asked, "Well, good chocolate is always a cure for that. What can I get for you?"

"Oh, I don't want chocolate," Jacqui shot back, her tone hiking. "I'm doing a high-protein diet to stay in shape for summer. Of course, you don't have to pay attention to that with your long dresses, do you, dear?"

One, two, three...

"What I'm calling about is your apartment. I'd like to rent it."

Her apartment?

Meg frowned. The second floor of her house held two apartments: cute, clean and in good shape after years of plaster dust, plumbing and paint. She lived in one and rented the other. Her most recent tenants had moved out in mid-May after graduating from Meg's alma mater, Alfred University. But why would Jacqui Crosby want her apartment, and how on Earth could Meg tell her no?

"Brad and Denise are having a house built outside of Hornell," Jacqui continued. "Their old place is too small with the new baby on the way and they need a place to stay for the summer. My kitchen's being redone and you know what a mess remodeling is, so there's no way I can have Brad Junior running around underfoot for eight weeks. How much is the rent?"

Brad and Denise, staying next door all summer,

with the little boy they conceived while she wore Brad's ring?

"Jacqui, I'm sorry, it's not available. And it's a small unit," Meg added. "It wouldn't suit them."

"Oh, but it would," the older woman insisted. "I expect they'd do nothing more than sleep there, Megan, and spend the days over here while Brad worked."

Megan had heard enough of the local gossip to know Denise wasn't a big fan of Jacqui's interfering nature. There was no chance the young mother would spend day after day at the Crosbys while Brad worked. No, she'd be here, hanging out, a visible reminder of what kind of girl actually got the guy in the end. And it wasn't the petticoat-wearing business woman with a candy store. Oh, no. It was the blond fashion doll sporting tight jeans, tight shirts and no job.

Nope. Not going to happen. "I'm sorry, Jacqui, it's not possible and I've got to go. I've got chocolate on."

"But—"

But nothing. Meg recradled the phone, realized she'd been just short of rude and vowed to scan the caller ID more carefully in the future. Regardless, no way, no how was she about to rent her next-door apartment to Brad and Denise, but Brad's mother kept her fingers on the town pulse, and Meg's ad in the weekly paper was hitting the stands today. She could only pray for a quick lease before Jacqui realized she'd been played, because that possible scenario wouldn't bode well for anyone.

Danny scanned the day-old classified list, frowned and headed back to his rental car. He climbed in, started the engine, studied the map and his directions from Google, missing the GPS on his Beemer but not willing to have his car mark him as a man with money.

Making a K-turn, he headed south and west to view this last apartment. With any luck, he might be able to move in tomorrow. Get established. That would be perfect.

His phone jangled the opening notes to "My Boy Lollipop," his sister's signature ringtone, an inside joke among the Romesser clan. They'd agreed to use candy songs to identify themselves, including Grandma Mary, making the quirk totally childish but fun. Danny hit the speakerphone button, in no mood for a traffic ticket for not being hands free. "Hey, sis. What's up?"

"Can we change places?"

He bit back the phrase *in a heartbeat,* wanting to help her. But he couldn't, and that cut into his protective instincts. "What's going on?"

"Trouble in Philly at the University City location."

Ouch. That particular Philly store had been problematic lately; a string of small thefts and possible gang influence had targeted their location adjacent to the University of Pennsylvania campus. "Do we need additional security?"

"Done. I amped up the internal monitoring and didn't tell the staff, but I feel like a spy, watching them like this."

"All it takes is one bad apple, Mary Clare. One dishonest person can totally ruin your bottom line and set a store up for failure. You know that."

"You're right, of course, it's just a weird feeling. The security agency will be doing the hands-on video scan so I feel slightly less intrusive."

Danny understood the dilemma. Security was an unfortunate necessity, more so in certain locales, and Mary Clare hadn't overseen those venues as yet. Time and circumstance had gotten in the way. He broached that subject cautiously. "Are you doing okay, Mare?"

"Mostly."

Danny cringed, wanting to help, knowing there was nothing he could do.

"I'm keeping busy. Working here actually helps, it keeps me away from places that Christian and I used to go to. A few degrees of separation isn't a bad thing right now."

"And you know you can call me anytime, right?" Danny was stating the obvious since she'd just called, but her vulnerability called to the guardian in him. Plus Philly had been dealing with an upswing in violent crimes lately, not exactly the setting he'd normally choose for his younger sister. "About anything."

"I know." She breathed a tiny sigh and hesitated for long ticks of the clock before adding, "This is good for me."

Danny heard the silent exception. "But?"

"It's hard."

"I know." They'd buried her fiancé less than a year before, an army officer killed in a roadside bombing in Afghanistan. "I miss him, too."

"He'd get a kick out of you being tucked in the foothills of Appalachia. You know that, don't you?"

"Yes, I do. But no more so than my friends who make it a point to text me about their weekend plans in the big city."

"Harsh."

Danny laughed. "It's pretty here, though." The word pretty conjured up mental images of Megan Russo. Danny shut them out. "And if you're doing okay, and it sounds like you are, I've got to hang up because I'm about to look at an apartment that sounds ideal."

"Wonderful. Thanks for being my sounding board. Again."

He smiled, wanting her to succeed, knowing he'd be there at a moment's notice to help if she floundered, because that was what brothers did. "Anytime, sis."

Chapter Four

Twenty minutes later Danny trudged back to his car, totally frustrated, fighting a headache and a suspicion he might be infested. The state of that garage apartment left a lot to be desired, and he was pretty sure he'd spied a colony of silverfish beneath the sink, while the faint but lingering smell of a dead mouse wafted from a west-facing wall.

At this moment the motel he'd booked for the night was looking better and better.

He stopped to gas up and withdrew a fresh edition of the small weekly paper from a rack inside the convenience store, pleasantly surprised when the cashier waved off the two-quarter price. "We just give them away, sir. You have a nice day, now."

The young man's easy nature brightened Danny's smile. And the giveaway policy was good business for advertisers. He pulled into a parking space, opened the half size newspaper, noted a full-page ad advertising an upcoming balloon rally and mentally logged in the date.

His grandfather had been a hot air balloon pilot, and he'd taught Danny the skills early on. If all went well and time allowed, Danny had every intention of having his balloon trucked down to Allegany County. Taking part in the local ballooning event would be his reward for a job well done.

He flipped back a few pages and scanned the classifieds for new listings. Most were long-term apartments or homes, but his gaze trained on one advertisement. "Available now, immaculate one-bedroom, full bath, galley kitchen, furnished, priced right, short- or long-term lease considered."

He withdrew his phone, got a clear tone and dialed the number, hopeful.

"Hello."

"Good evening, my name is Daniel Graham and I'm calling about your ad in the paper. The one for the immaculate one-bedroom apartment. Is it still available? And is it really, truly immaculate? Because I'd be okay with that."

Silence. Absolute, utter silence.

Danny tried again. "Hello?" He pulled the phone from his ear, saw the bars that said he was still connected and frowned. "Hello? Are you there?"

A sigh echoed through the phone. "I'm here. I… umm…"

"I can get references if you like," Danny offered,

trying to sweeten the deal. "I'm in town on business this summer and need a place to stay, so I'm looking at short-term. Eight to twelve weeks, most likely. Would that be all right?"

Another silence descended before he heard another sigh, but there was something about that soft sigh, that voice…

Obviously he needed food and a good night's sleep when he started recognizing a stranger's voice on the phone. "May I come see it?"

"Now?"

"I'm available. It's in Jamison?"

"Yes."

"And I'm just around the corner on Route 19. Can you give me the address? If this is a good time, of course," he hastened to add, realizing he was steamrolling the woman. The first thing he'd decided upon arriving in town was that these people weren't the kind to appreciate hardball tactics. New York, Boston, Baltimore, Philly… Those venues admired a guy who got the job done with as few words and left turns as possible.

Here? Not so much.

He pressed more gently. "If tomorrow would be better…"

"Now's fine."

Relief eased the tightness of his shoulders. "You're sure?"

"Yes. Come on by."

"But where are you? What's the address?"

"Oh, you're sure to find it, no problem. You were here just a few hours ago."

He was—

"Miss Russo?"

"Yes."

She didn't sound thrilled. Perhaps a touch resigned or fatalistic, as if life had just handed her a worst-case scenario.

Which would be the case if he put her and her cute little store out of business. But he couldn't think about that now. Surely there were prime locations far enough away from her store that their ventures could coexist. Wellsville was a good bit south. And it was a tribute store they were talking, not one of their sprawling big-city venues. Down here they were envisioning a smaller edition, a nod of thanks to the hometown of Grandma Mary's Candies, now a multi-million-dollar-per-year enterprise. A welcome addition to the struggling economy.

But Danny was fresh out of choices, so he swallowed the nugget of guilt and thrust the car into gear. "I'm on my way."

"Wonderful." She didn't sound like she thought it was all that wonderful, but at least she was open to the idea of showing him the place. And it couldn't be as bad as what he'd just seen. Could it?

"The entrance to the apartment is around back. I'll be there."

"See you in a few minutes."

* * *

Megan clipped her hair back, smoothed damp palms against her blue jeans and headed downstairs at a quick clip. He must have really been just around the corner because his car pulled into the small parking area as she opened the door. He climbed out, a lightweight zip-up jacket giving him an upper-class look that didn't exactly jibe with his discount-label jeans and pullover. He strode forward, looking just as good as he had short hours before, sunglasses hiding his eyes until he stood two steps beneath her, tipped the glasses up and gave her a once-over. "Wow."

While she appreciated the one-word observation, she'd been "wowed" before, only to crash in total ignominy. She met his gaze, stomped down the spike of her heartbeat and jerked her head toward the back door. "The apartment's up here."

"I'm right behind you."

Oh, she knew that, all right. It was written on his face and evident in the sparks jumping between them, but she'd learned to evade electricity. She ignored the hint of appreciation in his voice but noted it was just enough to make the tone almost meaningful. Too much labeled a guy a total come-on. Too little meant he was probably inept and needy. Danny's voice was neither. It was…perfect.

But she had no use for men passing through town on business. Since she'd become the head of the Jamison Broken Hearts Society, membership of one, she'd grown smart enough to be jaded without appearing jaded. A good trick.

"It's small," she told him over her shoulder.

"Small works. It's easier to keep clean."

She stepped inside the upper door. "This is it. Living room, kitchen, bedroom, bath."

He nodded, his gaze scanning the area, his emotions shielded. She couldn't tell if he liked or hated the place, and that meant he had practice hiding emotions. Not a good sign. He stepped inside, moved forward, then paused overlong. "It's spotless."

She frowned. "I do believe the ad mentioned that."

He turned and flashed a grin that made her heart quiver and her gut tingle, two physical reactions she'd just as soon chalk up to lack of iron. She was definitely in danger of being swept away by that smile. Those eyes. And great teeth, besides. Her mother was a dental hygienist in the lone dental office in Wellsville. She'd fall in love with those teeth, right off.

"It did. But the last one I looked at said 'clean' and it wasn't even close. I'll take it."

"You don't want to know the rent?"

"If it's too high, I'll wrangle it down. But somehow, since it's you, I'm expecting the price will be fair."

Of course it was fair. She would never consider bilking someone out of too much money for her own gain, or conniving her way into anything. For just a moment she lamented the idea of being good, of taking God's word to heart and soul, and considered smacking him with an outrageous price so he'd take his appreciative gaze and business-savvy self elsewhere. She hesitated, wishing she could do that, knowing she couldn't. "Six hundred a month. Plus utilities."

"Done." He stuck out a hand. "Do you have a lease handy?"

She nodded. "On my side. Come this way." She led the way back down the stairs and around to a second entrance. She opened the door and proceeded up the inner stairway to a slightly more spacious apartment than his. She watched as he glanced around, surprised. "I expected different."

"Than?"

He waved a hand. "This. This is fun. Modern. Kind of funky."

She eyed the mix of bright-toned pillows, flowers and casual corduroy seating, then laughed at the expression on his face. "You thought I'd have a wood-burning stove, perhaps? A spindle? A straw mattress on the wood floor?"

He grinned, then shrugged. "An understandable mistake, Miss Russo. And might I add you look just as good in denim as you did in calico."

"Normal men don't know materials. You realize that, right?"

He flashed the smile again, the one that appeared open and honest, engaging and appealing. Key word: *appeared*.

"My grandmother quilts. Beautiful stuff. She uses

calico and ginghams a lot. And plain colors. But she's partial to calico."

Megan nodded. So was she, truth be told. But it would seem weird to deck out her apartment in too many old-fashioned things. Like she was caught in the past or something.

A house would be different. Someday she'd live in a sweet old colonial that hadn't been split into multiple units, raise a bunch of kids, bake cookies, make candy for her own brood and welcome her husband home every night.

She faced Danny. "Rent is due by the first of the month."

He grinned. "Which makes me late already. Here you go." He bent and filled out a check drawn on a local bank. She frowned and raised an eyebrow toward him.

"You don't live here."

"No, but I opened a local account for business purposes before I came down. Makes things easier because, as you noted this morning, not every business down here uses plastic."

She accepted the check, scanned the amount, noted that it was for two months and gave him a brisk nod. "Thank you, Mr. Graham."

He edged closer. "My friends call me Danny."

She refused to budge despite his proximity, tilted her head up and met the undisguised twinkle in his gaze. Oh, yes, this boy had been around a bit. Or maybe she was becoming an old cynic like Mrs.

Dennehy, the grocer's aged mother. She bit back a sigh, met his gaze with an equanimity she didn't feel and angled her head slightly, knowing that maneuver had caught his attention earlier. "But we're not friends."

He nodded toward the check and grinned. "We might be in two months. Wouldn't hurt to get in practice, Miss Russo. After all, we *are* going to be neighbors."

And that was all they'd be. She'd make certain of that. She nodded and moved toward the door, refusing to feel trapped over something as simple as a name. Besides, he was right. They'd be living side by side for eight weeks. She gave him an over-the-shoulder glance as she descended the stairs, noting his approval seemed just as notable going down the stairs. "Megan. My friends call me Meg."

"And Ben calls you Meggie."

She nodded and glanced back again, but this time held his look. "He's the *only* one that calls me that. Got it?"

His grin deepened. "Got it. Can I move in tomorrow?"

She withdrew a key from her front pocket and dangled it in front of him. "Whatever works for you." She stuck out a hand once he accepted the key and flashed him a smile. "Welcome to Jamison."

His grip was strong and firm. She refused to acknowledge the sweet spark of awareness that traveled up her arm and through her chest, nestling somewhere cozy in her belly. He held her hand a little longer than could ever be considered necessary and dipped his chin in acknowledgement when he let it go. "Thank you. It's nice to be here."

Chapter Five

"Yowza."

Meg shot Hannah a warning look the next afternoon. "Stop."

"He's moving in?"

"How's that nut chopping coming, Hannah? You done yet?"

"Today?"

"Hannah Moore…"

"Got it." Hannah ducked beneath the counter, withdrew a tub of toasted almonds and filled the food processor halfway. She hit On, and the ensuing noise stopped conversation until the nuts were evenly chopped to her satisfaction. She dumped the cylinder into a bowl and then repeated the process twice more. Stepping back, she eyed the bowl and the chocolate vat, then nodded. "We're good."

"Thanks. Measure out three cups of those for the toffee, and we'll be just about there."

"Wonderful."

The half wall and Dutch door made it easy to keep an eye on the store. The old-fashioned bell over the door helped, too, an old-school way of announcing a customer when Megan's attention was diverted. Hannah set the three cups aside in a smaller bowl and glanced out the window. "A customer."

"You got it?"

"I do."

Megan swept her chocolate-dotted apron a quick glance as the door chime announced what Hannah already knew, her warm voice mingling with others as the tourists exclaimed over this and that.

It was early yet. Midweek mornings were traditionally quiet while tourists walked, climbed, went sightseeing and shopping. Since chocolate didn't do well in cars on a warm summer day, the candy store was generally their last stop before heading home or back to the motels in nearby Wellsville. That meant Meg made good use of the mornings, both before and after the shop opened, then busied herself with customers the rest of the day. And her ice cream window business was steady from three o'clock on, especially when area kids had summer sports in the evening. Then the line could grow ridiculously long in a relatively short space of time.

She'd hired a local college girl, Crystal Murphy, to help out part-time and had two more college girls consigned to run her weekend festival booths. Coupled with Hannah's summer-shortened library hours, they should be all right.

When Hannah returned to the kitchen, she met Meg's gaze and swept the departing family a wistful look. "They had the cutest baby."

"Yeah?"

"Yes." Hannah checked the toffee bar molds, nodded satisfaction, then tipped her gaze Megan's way. "What's that look for?"

Megan shrugged. "I hate being in my thirties."

"Stupid biological clock?"

"Exactly. As much fun as this all is—" Megan waved a hand around the white kitchen "—it's not exactly what I'd planned for this stage in my life."

"Something that included a cute and loving husband, a couple of kids, a kitchen of your own and a cozy fire on long winter nights?"

"Bingo. I'm not even close to anything like that, and I can't help but wonder why. Is it me? Them? Are men different from what they were before?"

"Umm. Asking the wrong girl. I'd kind of decided that was beyond the realm of possibilities before I moved here. Mostly I'm okay with that."

"Should I ask why?"

"Probably not. I could tell you, but then I'd have to kill you." Something in Hannah's tone, or maybe it was her bearing, made the words more poignant and less funny, but Megan refused to pry.

"A need-to-know basis." She nodded, laughing. "I get it. Obviously the witness protection program is using Jamison, New York, as a current venue."

Hannah tipped an amused look Megan's way. "Yup. My real name is a state secret."

"Since I love the name Hannah, you may keep it a state secret."

"Does it bug you, Megan? To have been that close to marriage twice and have it fall apart?"

Megan weighed her answer as she watched the toffee mixture darken and condense. "If by 'bug' you mean have my episodes of public humiliation turned me off members of the opposite sex for the duration of my natural life, I'd have to say that's understandable, considering the circumstances."

"Michael was a jerk."

"I know. And so was Brad. But the turnaround of that is—why do I attract jerks? Am I so needy that I latch on to any Tom, Dick or Harry that comes along?"

"So if my name was Tom, Dick or Harry, you might give me a chance?"

Megan stopped stirring the boiling toffee mix, mortified.

Danny stood at the back door to the kitchen, looking way too amused and sure of himself for anyone's good, particularly hers.

"Eavesdropping is against the lease rules," she said.

He waved a careless hand to the open door. "You weren't exactly quiet. I could hear you in the yard."

Hannah tried to mask a laugh, unsuccessfully. She shot him a look as she removed a tray of supersize cookies from the oven, set it down and replaced it with another. "He's right. I forgot he was out there. Sorry."

Danny leaned his elbows against the metal brace separating the upper screen from the window below. "Back to my question…"

"No."

"You're sure? I could change my name."

"Listen, I'm working right now, and toffee has a mind of its own. As much as I'd love nothing better than to grow old sparring with you, the likelihood of that is zero. So if you'd be so kind as to maintain a proper landlord/tenant relationship at all times, we'll both be better off."

"I get it."

He might have gotten it, but he didn't look all that dissuaded. Great. Just her luck to have rented that apartment to someone who liked a challenge. Megan had no intention of challenging anyone, at least not anyone in the near future. Hadn't Reverend Hannity talked about God's plan just last week, the road less traveled, the unexpected twists, turns and inevitable forks along the way?

Megan wasn't sure where her road forked, but she was pretty certain that Danny Graham's fork would zag left in about eight weeks, and she was determined to stand stalwart and solid for that time.

She tested the toffee texture by dropping a tiny bit into a cup of cold water, fingered the texture to assess brittleness, then examined the threads dangling from the spoon. Her practiced eye told her this batch was done. She set it off the burner, maneuvered the handle left, hoisted the pan and gently poured a thin stream into the bar molds.

"You don't use a candy thermometer?"

"No."

"Why?"

"Unreliable."

"And that…maneuver, the thing with the water cup and the spoon, wasn't?"

"Not if you know what you're doing."

Danny knew what he was doing. Always had. He'd been raised to make candy in a state-of-the-art facility that believed in small batches, but each batch was expertly measured and timed to assure the quality of the mix. Watching her, he had a vision of what his great-grandmother must have done on her porch outside Wellsville, the little house, long since gone, that had been the original home of Mary Sandoval's Candies.

Hannah moved along the cooling molds, sifting chopped nuts onto the surface, then using a wooden board to press them into the cooling toffee. An interesting thought crept into Danny's head, of how cool it would be to do candy demonstrations like this at the tribute store, to show people the origins of his company, the skills required before automated machinery replaced the hands-on techniques he'd just witnessed. He stayed silent a moment, watching them work, then cleared his throat.

"You're still here."

"Watching and waiting."

She sighed, just enough to let him know she wanted him gone. "What?"

"Do I need to call the electric company and have things put in my name?"

"Oh." She paused, chagrined, as if she'd been rude by ignoring him. Which she had, of sorts, but from what he'd overheard, she had good reason to shy away from men who appeared too good to be true. Although he had to seriously doubt the intelligence of the locals if they took one look at the incredibly delightful woman before him, her curly hair somewhat tamed in a crocheted hairnet, and her gold-plaid floor-length dress a nod of appreciation to simpler times. He almost felt the comfort of that when he was in her presence.

Almost.

She turned his way once the pot was empty, set it in a big, deep utility sink, turned on the hot water to melt the sugary coating and moved his way. "Sorry. I should have told you that. They'll send the bill to me and I'll pass it to you. For long-term leases I transfer it to the tenant's name, but there's no sense doing that for eight weeks. Is that all right?"

"It's fine." She had a smear of milk chocolate along her lower cheek, and her apron bore similar traces of her work. The dress, from what he could see, appeared spotless. He waved in that direction. "Won't you get that messed up back here? In the kitchen?"

She nodded and shrugged. "Necessity. Women in the eighteen hundreds didn't have the choice of wearing blue jeans and pullovers. They had to deal with all this, and when I wait on customers I like to be in costume. That helps steer conversation to candy making like it was." She arched a brow and lifted a shoulder. "They learn more, then buy more."

"Crafty."

She nodded, opened the screen door and stepped out onto the small back porch. "Yes and no. I really like teaching, it's in my blood, but I love candy making. I started doing this as a child and it comes easily to me. This way I can combine the two. And I do freelance work at the Genesee Country Museum in Livonia, too. For their special weekends we do candy-making demonstrations on-site. People love it."

He could envision that, no problem, seeing her like this, in her candy kitchen, comfortable in her element. On impulse he reached out his left hand and used his thumb to wipe away the dab of chocolate.

She stepped back, startled out of her comfort zone.

He raised his hand. "You had chocolate on your cheek. Well, chin, actually."

"You could have just told me."

He grinned and put up both hands, palms out, as if surrendering. "More fun this way. So…" The look on her face told him a change of subject was in order. He took the hint. "I've moved in and I'm grateful for the chance to be out of the motel. Since we're in fairly close proximity—"

Her gaze puckered, purposely.

He chose to ignore the chagrin. "And we're going to see one another regularly..."

She mock-scowled, exaggerated for his benefit, a look that said, *Get to the point, bud, I've got work to do...*

"I thought I'd ask you to please let me know if I do anything to disturb you. I don't want to be a thorn in your side, and since my name is Daniel and not Tom, Dick or Harry—"

A flush mounted her cheeks.

"—I'll do my best to stay on my side of the Great Divide. Okay?"

She sighed, looked like she was struggling mightily to bring her feelings in line, gazed beyond him then drew her look back, reluctance shadowing the movement. "You're my tenant. I'm your temporary landlord. You are welcome to come over here any time. I just..."

He moved a half step closer, noting the smattering of freckles seemed darker in the midday sun, that the tendrils of gold-brown hair escaping the net were two shades lighter than the rest of her hair and that her mouth was an indescribable shade of pink.

She bit her lip, looked up and must have read something in his eyes, because she drew a breath, pasted an easy smile of dismissal on her face and stepped back inside. "Now that we have that clear…"

"Crystal."

"Absolutely. Yes." She nodded toward the kitchen. "I've got to get back to work."

"As do I."

"Well, then…" She sounded almost reluctant to return to her duties, which was exactly how Danny felt about returning to his. Smarter for both if they ignored their obvious attraction by maintaining some distance.

He headed down the steps. "Nice talking with you, ladies."

"Right."

He grinned, recognizing the note of indecision in her voice, and wishing he could hear the feminine exchange slated to take place, but he had work to do. So did she.

As he climbed into his car, he remembered how she looked in that kitchen, cheeks pink from the heat, her gorgeous hair tucked beneath the old-fashioned crocheted hairnet. Try as he might, he hadn't been able to get her out of his mind. And for some odd reason, he really didn't want to.

But propriety told him Megan was off-limits. He had the advantage of knowing why he was in town, of understanding how his business moves could affect her livelihood. He couldn't take that lightly.

Plus his parents wouldn't take kindly to him toying with anyone's affections. Despite his worldly experience, Danny wasn't a player. He chose not to be, out of respect for his parents and his faith. In his travel-savvy world, that was a big difference, and while he'd fallen away from church attendance in his global wanderings, he hadn't shrugged off the reality of a higher power, a Supreme Being. He just hoped God was the patient sort while he worked to build their candy business. Their coming Christmas catalog was crammed full of chocolate decadence. Its success would be a major step forward, a feather in his cap if it took off as he projected.

But he should leave sweet Megan alone. She seemed like the kind of girl who deserved nothing but the best, a guy who would be home day after day, the American dream of home and family she'd talked about so openly. Danny's job kept him in the field so much that he was rarely in any one place for too long.

Home. The idea of starting a home had once seemed alien to him, an impossibility, one of those things that happened to other guys. And while several of his friends had married recently, several others were still footloose, and that had been fine because Danny hadn't felt that spark, that hint of happily-ever-after possibilities.

Until now. With a woman completely off-limits. What was the good Lord thinking?

Chapter Six

Three days later Megan was contemplating the likelihood of being arrested for peeking out a window, watching for her neighbor's return, totally wrong behavior that felt strangely right.

She'd obviously crossed a line. She definitely needed to leave her neighbor alone. Absolutely, positively alone.

Then why had she left a welcome basket of assorted cookies on his doorstep an hour before?

Simple. She was a glutton for punishment with little self-discipline.

Or she was a great neighbor. She brightened at the thought. That was what people did, right? They offered a welcome to their new neighbors, inviting them to be part of the community? Of course they did.

Nevertheless, Megan was still determined to keep her distance from Danny, but if he came over to thank her for the cookies, she'd be nice. Sweet. Friendly.

You are so in trouble, and the guy just got here. What are you thinking?

That was just it. She was trying so hard *not* to think about him that she was constantly thinking about him. A bad sign. Really bad. His footsteps down the back stairs made her breath hitch, wondering if he would turn right, toward her door, or left, toward the driveway.

He'd gone left, every day, just like she'd asked him to, but that didn't stop her heart from skittering every time she heard him pull into the driveway, the quiet engine and the car door closing marking his presence late in the day.

So now she was tempting him across the divide with homemade baked goods. What on Earth was she thinking?

"Megan, you here?"

"Alyssa." Meg stepped through the candy kitchen door and beamed at her married, very pregnant friend. "Oh, my gosh, look at you. I don't see you for two weeks and you—"

"Popped." Alyssa hugged Megan, then laughed and passed a hand over six months of baby. "That's what the locals are calling it."

"Perfect." Megan stood back, perused Alyssa, then grinned and nodded. "You look so happy."

Alyssa's smile confirmed Meg's assertion. "I really am. I should feel guilty about being this delighted with life."

"No, you shouldn't." Megan offered her best scolding look, very nineteenth century. "You deserve to be happy. God gives us chances. Our job is to either take that chance or duck and run. You took the chance and happiness was just one of the fringe benefits. How's Cory doing?" Cory was Alyssa's four-year-old daughter from a former marriage. The precocious preschooler had been hospitalized the previous summer with a heart condition, a scary time for Alyssa's family and the entire town.

"She's wonderful. You'd never know she'd had problems, to look at her, and she's got Trent and Jaden wrapped around her little finger. I'm hoping some of that will ease once this baby arrives to give her a little competition."

"Then Trent can spoil them all," Megan noted. "Have you got time for coffee? Say yes, please."

"Yes," Alyssa laughed. "How about you?" She motioned toward the production area.

"Yup." Meg headed into the kitchen and grabbed a couple of mugs. "I've got the morning work done and it's quiet until two or so, so this is the perfect time to chat. I can't believe we live ten minutes apart and I haven't seen you in two weeks. Are you in a Chocolate Glazed Donut coffee mood, French Vanilla or straight?"

"Chocolate. Always. And gainful employment and family stuff manage to steal time, don't they?" Alyssa smiled her approval when Megan backed through the swinging half door with two mugs of flavored coffee.

"Oh, yum." Alyssa leaned forward, breathed deep, and relaxed into her chair. "This is lovely."

Megan laughed. "It is. And you look marvelous."

"Thank you. I'm not quite to beached-whale stage yet, so I'll accept your compliment graciously. In six weeks, I may bite your head off, so be forewarned."

"I'll take it under consideration. Are you helping staff the restaurant's booth for the Balloon Rally?" Alyssa's family owned and managed The Edge in Jamison, a gracious hilltop restaurant that overlooked the valley, now doubling as a wedding reception and special-occasion hot spot. Alyssa's mother made to-die-for strudels, and the family sold them at a rally booth every year.

Alyssa nodded. "Absolutely. It will be fun. I kept that weekend clear of weddings because it's silly to overbook and drive the servers crazy. We've got to have enough people on-site for the rally to bake and serve, and who wants to miss the balloons or fight traffic to do a wedding on Balloon Rally weekend?"

"Good point. And there's only so much you can handle at this stage of pregnancy, right?"

Alyssa shot her a look of disbelief. "Unfortunately, once you've got a kid, that scenario goes out the window. You hit the ground running once they're born and you don't look back. Trent keeps telling me to slow down, but I feel…" She sighed, smiling. "Wonderful."

"You're married to one of the greatest guys on Earth, have a beautiful home perfect for raising babies and a job running a great restaurant. I'd say you have reason to feel wonderful."

"I agree." Alyssa sat forward and grasped Megan's hand. "And I wish the same for you. I heard that Brad and Denise were coming into town this week, and I had to hold myself back from going over to Jacqueline's house and having it out with them."

"Old news."

"It still hurts."

Megan shrugged. "It really doesn't. Not anymore. Oh, don't get me wrong." She met Alyssa's raised brow with a half smile. "I don't like the fact that they're going to be underfoot all summer, but I really wish them well. It was a long time ago and I hope they're happy together. And Brad did me a favor." She sent a knowing look Alyssa's way. "You and I both know that."

"And Michael?"

"Grrr…" Megan mock scowled. "He did, too, but that whole left-at-the-altar thing? So not cool. My parents still go ballistic thinking about it, but I heard gossip that he's cheating on his new girlfriend over at Alfred State, so again, it's just as well. I've read half a dozen self-help books, and the conclusion is that I need to up my standards considerably. Not trade down."

"I won't disagree there, and you're better off without Michael. We all know that." Alyssa squeezed her hand and leaned forward, her look empathetic. "But more than anything, I want you happy."

"Like you."

She beamed. "Exactly like me. So we can raise our kids together. Coach soccer teams. Watch football under the lights while we eat hamburgers grilled by our husbands for the Sports Boosters' Fund."

"Smalltown, USA."

"But good."

Megan sighed. "It is good, but pretty unreachable. It's not like Jamison and Wellsville are overflowing with a truckload of available thirty-somethings dying to settle down. Most of the available guys are unmarried for good reason."

Alyssa contemplated that, then nodded. "Unfortunately, you're right. But they're not the only game in town, I hear." She slid her gaze left. "I understand we got a new tenant last week."

"Life in a small town."

"Oh, yes. Not much gets by people here. But in this case, the rumor mill has taken a very positive slant on this newcomer."

"He's...nice."

"Nice?" Alyssa's furrowed brow invited more.

"And funny."

"Humor in a man is a wonderful thing. It almost makes them palatable. Tell me more."

Megan squirmed. "That's it. He's here for eight weeks on business, has a great smile. Not too tall, but tall enough that I look up to him."

"Oh, really?"

"Stop. He's just a tenant. And I've scarcely seen him. But he's got great eyes."

"Does he now?" Alyssa leaned forward, heightened interest arching her brows, lighting her eyes. "Do you think he's good-looking? Because I've heard he's hot enough to burn toast in a microwave."

Megan laughed, considered, then nodded. "I can't disagree, although your analogy's a little strange. And he's smart. Quick-witted. And totally off-limits."

"Why?"

Megan raised her hands up. "Let's backtrack to the 'here for eight weeks' part of the conversation. He leaves. I stay. I don't need another bout of heartache, particularly in the public view again. Seriously, Lyssa, cut me some slack, okay? Once was hard. Twice was torture. No way in this world am I going for a third round. Uh-uh. I'm doing strategic planning to keep my heart intact."

Alyssa nodded, her lips pressed into a tight line. "I can understand that. But it seems that sometimes, despite our best plans, God has other ideas."

"My present plan is to build my business and lay

low until the sting of Michael's rejection moves to a back row of my mind. Oh, and figure out how to help my parents manage Ben's quirks. Has he been okay at the restaurant?"

Alyssa nodded. "He always is. He saves the shenanigans for his family."

Megan weighed that and shrugged. "It's good that he discerns the difference, but it's not easy to have a grown man who thinks preschool pranks are funny."

"You're right. Are your parents still considering moving him into a group home?"

"Dad is. Mom won't hear of it. And that's probably part of the problem. She feels like she's abandoning him, while Dad thinks it would be good for him. The group home outside of Wellsville would shuttle him to work every day, and they take the residents to movies, shopping, area events. Ben's high-functioning enough that he'd be fine with all that. He'd only be fifteen minutes from home, so we could grab him for supper or weekends whenever we wanted, but Mom keeps saying no."

"A standoff."

"Yes."

Alyssa drained her coffee and stood. "That's not easy, Meg. But I can see both sides. Your mother feels responsible and it's hard to give that up. But your Dad is looking at what's best for Ben long-term."

"Exactly."

"I'm tucking the whole matter onto my prayer list. And you." Alyssa reached out and hugged Megan. "I want you happy. And I wish I could roll time back and make Michael and Brad just disappear from the whole picture. I don't want their negativity to mess up chances you might have taken otherwise."

Megan sidled a glance Alyssa's way as she walked her to the door. "Meaning don't ignore the cute guy next door because you've been burned at the stake on the town square twice."

"Not burned. Singed. There's a difference."

"Semantics, Lyssa. But for the moment, I've got all I can handle just trying to maintain and not get bogged down in the whys and hows of the situation. I was just as much at fault as they were."

"Not true. Not even close to true."

Megan laid a hand on Alyssa's arm. "It is. At least partially. I wanted the dream. Wanted it so badly that I let myself think Brad was the real deal. He wasn't. And then Michael. I should have called a halt to that long before he proposed, and then I was in too deep. He did us both a favor. Big time."

"Well, he could have done it a few days earlier." Alyssa rolled her eyes. "But God's got better things in store for you. And I've got to get to the preschool and grab Cory. We're meeting Trent for lunch at the Beef Haus."

Megan gave her a quick hug. "Thanks for stopping by. Tweaking me."

Alyssa returned the embrace. "You're doing fine.

I know that. But when I found out Brad was coming into town for the summer, I got mad. Protective."

Megan grinned. "I like it when my girlfriends watch my back. I'm okay with that." She said good-bye as two cars angled into the little parking lot abutting the store. A variety of older women climbed out of each car, their back-and-forth chatter reminiscent of the finch house in the backyard. Megan waved a friendly greeting, waited on the broad porch, then held the door open as they stepped inside, exclaiming over this and that.

She had a business she loved and a family she cherished, and despite that goofy biological clock, she had time. She knew that. What she hated was not having control. That whole 'let go and let God' scenario that people talked about?

Tough for a girl that liked to make her own way in this world.

She followed the ladies inside and grinned while they browsed the counters, their delightful exchanges heralding old times. Old candies. Days gone by.

By the time they left, they'd bought several hundred dollars' worth of wonderful candies to take home to family and friends. A great start to a wonderful day.

Danny spotted the old-style basket at his front door, filled with individually wrapped huge cookies, the kind every little kid longs for, including the little boy that lingered in this grown man's body. He seized the basket, realized it was long past supper time and scoured the contents for a note. The mid-June day was bright despite the evening hour.

No note.

He sighed, scratched his head, frowned and glanced around the corner toward Meg's back door. He'd passed a long line of ice cream customers at the front, the regular *clomp, clomp* of feet on the wide wooden steps an old-fashioned sound in keeping with her business. He headed toward her back door, second-guessing his choice, but needing to be polite and thank her for the gift.

She very nearly whapped him in the face with the storm door as she lugged out a bag of garbage, mortification and surprise stressing her features when she spotted him there. "Danny, I'm sorry. I didn't see you. Are you okay?"

Was the note of concern a hint more personal than it needed to be?

The zigzag of his heart said yes.

Common sense said he was being ridiculous. She'd made her case clear the other day, a stand that made perfect sense for both of them.

And then left cookies at your door.

Neighborly, he decided, ignoring the internal warning. Very old-time friendly. With the cutest dimple just above the left side of her mouth.

"I'm fine. No harm done." He set down the cookie basket, grasped the garbage bag and hoisted the overloaded thing, then eyed it and her. "Does the idea of changing this more often not occur to you?"

She flushed then sighed, chagrined. "I should, I know. I tend to use things up. Wear them out."

"Frugal."

"Whereas I call it bottom-line conscious," she told him, following as he toted the heavy bag across the backyard. "But yes, I should have dumped it midday and I didn't. My bad."

"Waste not, want not." He faced her after tossing the bag into the Dumpster. "I've got a grandmother who spouts proverbs on a regular basis."

Megan acknowledged that with a knowing smile. "Don't we all?"

Her pretty smile made him wonder if she noticed how easily he'd handled the heavy bag, while his inner thoughts whacked him upside the head with the reality that he'd be leaving soon, and the gracious young woman standing before him didn't deserve to be left, ever again.

Obviously Brad and Michael were complete morons.

He nodded toward the cookie basket he'd set down. "No note?"

She flushed again. "I figured you'd know who they were from." Her shoulders rose in explanation as if convincing herself or him, possibly both. "I hadn't officially welcomed you to the neighborhood, and that's what people do around here."

"Which only makes Jamison nicer, something I'd considered impossible."

She considered his words, then waved toward Main Street. "While it's lovely in many respects, Jamison's got all the flaws of small-town living, but the perks outweigh those. Most days." She headed for her door, her manner suggesting she needed to return to work. "I'm glad you like the cookies."

He fell into step beside her. "Right now they look like supper."

You're leaving. She's staying. What part of this are you not getting?

"You haven't eaten?" Meg asked.

He shook his head. "Worked through it. I was going to grab something then didn't, which was fairly short-sighted because I was hungry, so when I got out of the car and found these on my door-step, I was one happy man." He bent and retrieved the basket of cookies, a part of him longing to ask her to go out with him once she'd closed the store in another hour. Grab a bite to eat. Talk. Laugh. From the crinkle lines framing her eyes, he knew Megan Russo laughed often, a trait he found appealing, but then there wasn't much about this woman he hadn't found appealing, which made applying the brakes tougher than it should have been. Way tougher. He raised the cookies into the air. "Thank you, Meg."

She dipped a curtsy, a move that candy-coated his heart, not even close to playing fair. "You're welcome, kind sir."

She started back into the store, the sounds of Crystal's and Hannah's voices mingling with that of a Little League team, a fun mix, totally summer.

He wanted to slow her escape, despite the noisy call of her business, the throng of young people on the front steps. Part of him yearned to linger, to dawdle, to enjoy the late-day sun, the chatter of birds, the excitement of little-boy voices heralding a great win.

But the reality of their lives intruded on his conscience. His job was to leave. Mary Clare's phone call reminded him that he might have to duck out at a moment's notice, that his sister's emotional state might not be up to the rigors of East Coast marketing and monitoring, even though he knew this challenge was good for her.

And good for him, he admitted, though he wouldn't necessarily want to confess that to his mother. The peace and quiet of this sweet community enticed him.

Or was the enticement the beautiful woman before him?

Both, he decided.

In any case he had a job to do, a job he loved, one that kept him on the road way too often. He moved back, smiled and hiked the cookies once more. "Thanks again."

"You're welcome."

He didn't wink. Didn't smile too wide, didn't angle his head and give her the slow, measured look that said too much. No. He turned and quietly walked away, pretending he hadn't been listening for her feet on the steps every morning, the jangle of the bell saying she'd entered the quaint store, the sounds of the back door banging shut as she and Hannah loaded the van with cookies going here, there and everywhere.

He'd faked disinterest the past few days, turning left when he wanted to turn right, quietly leaving when he wanted to stay and hear her voice, make her laugh, watch the expressions she made so well, faces that said she didn't mind being the center of attention except in matters of the heart.

Right there was reason enough to walk away, protecting them both, but how he wished he didn't have to.

Chapter Seven

Way too close for comfort.

That's what Danny Graham was, Meg decided the next morning, ignoring the predawn darkness. She yawned, stretched and headed into the production kitchen, needing to get ahead on cookies before the predicted midday heat. Even with Hannah's and Crystal's help, and the college girls she hired to run cookie and fudge stands at area festivals, the monumental summer production work got her up in the early hours and back to bed late, so she ought to be too tired to even think about Danny Graham.

Wrong.

Too busy?

Nope.

Too smart?

There you go, her conscience agreed, the inner voice sounding a little too pleased.

Meg ignored the hint of sarcasm and pushed thoughts of Danny aside, right until she heard the sound of his door opening, his footsteps on the stairs, trying to pretend she wasn't hoping he'd stop over, say good morning, smile at her, tease her.

The sound of his car engine nixed those hopes. Just as well, she knew, because she had no business thinking such things anyway.

"Meg?"

The sound of his voice surprised her, sending skitters of anticipation up her spine. She pasted a calm look on her face and headed toward the back door. "I thought you were gone."

He studied her, glanced toward the driveway and the running car, then angled his head as if he knew she'd been listening for him. But there was no way he could know that, so she chalked it up to her overactive imagination.

"I'm heading to Wellsville for the day and was wondering if you needed anything brought back later. I heard you up and about early—"

"I woke you?"

He shook his head. "I had work to do on the computer."

"But—"

"And once the cable company installs my service, you should really put a lock on your internet connection."

"You pirated my WiFi?"

"Temporarily. I'm not wired for it on my side and the store is, and I had to get some things done."

He didn't even have the decency to look guilty

or embarrassed that she'd called him out, and that was one more reason to stay far away from Danny Graham. The guy was way too sure of himself. Too composed. Too adorable. Too...

His expression turned questioning. "Why didn't you have it installed on both sides?"

She had an easy answer for that. "College kids are notorious for not paying their last month of bills. I didn't want to be bothered with June phone calls about April and May expenses."

"Understandable."

"And you're having cable installed in my house?"

"It's baseball season, Meg. I'm a Yankees fan. End of story."

A Yankees fan.

Meg's entire family loved the Yankees, with the exception of Uncle Bob, who was from Massachusetts, making his Boston allegiance understandable.

Meg bled pinstripe blue all summer long. "I would have had it connected for you. Sorry."

"No apology needed. As you can see, I didn't hesitate to do it myself."

She should find that annoying, but she didn't. She appreciated take-charge people. She strove for that trait herself so she admired it in others. "Are they billing you directly?"

"Yes, and I promise—" he crossed his heart, the childish move cute and endearing "—to pay my bills on time."

He…is…not…endearing. The internal voice droned the warning, as if knocking sense into her.

But he was. And engaging. Worse, he knew it. She saw it in the quiet gaze, the quick twinkle, the look that said a little too much when he glanced to her mouth, his gaze wondering.

Right now the screen door was her new BFF.

"I'm glad you told me and I don't think there's anything I need from Wellsville, but thanks for checking. This is one of those days when a forty-five-minute round-trip for something I should have on hand would stagnate the day."

He reached out a slip of paper. "My cell phone number. I know you've got it on the lease agreement, but you should program it into your phone. That way if you need anything…" He opened the screen door, and stood in front of her.

Uh-oh.

"Anything at all," he continued, the fleeting touch of his hand as he handed off the paper making her heart flutter. "Give me a call."

Meg accepted the paper, shut down the quiver, gave Danny a businesslike nod and let the door shut of its own accord. "That's so nice of you, Danny. Thanks. I will."

His expression didn't change but his eyes said he read the pleasant dismissal for the self-defense mechanism it was. He didn't choose to challenge it, though.

He moved down the two steps and she breathed

easier. The trouble was, she liked the way she felt when he came around. When he smiled. Talked. Laughed.

He doffed a pretend cap.

She curtsied. The old-fashioned act softened his gaze, her hint of whimsy pleasing him.

"See you later." His look said he'd like to linger, but he had responsibilities. So did she. As she stepped back into the kitchen, she couldn't help scanning the wall clock, wondering what time he'd get home when he hadn't even left the driveway yet.

Do not look at that clock. Do not estimate the hours until you see him again. Put him out of your mind forthwith. Please.

She couldn't, which meant one thing.

Megan Russo was in big trouble, trouble she couldn't handle right now or maybe ever. From now on it would be no listening, no looking, shoulders back, chin up, her business-minded mentality fully engaged. Now, if only she could keep it that way when he was around.

Meg fit here, Danny decided, as he wandered the small streets of Jamison's business district late that afternoon. The stone-paved roads, flanked by historic architecture, offered a mix of old and new products in their old-world setting.

He'd spent the day culling possible sites for the tribute store, examining traffic patterns and town records. Wellsville was clearly the go-to place, and from a business perspective he loved the small-town feel of Main Street balanced by adequate parking and a welcoming ambiance. There were no available east-facing storefronts at the moment, so he'd need to examine things further, see if anyone needed or wanted to sell, but he felt good about the location, and in any good business plan, location was key.

Right now he wanted to acclimate himself with Jamison, admiring the mission of the town to attract tourists with old-world charm.

The Quiltin' Bee drew his attention. Grandma loved to quilt, and the shaded sidewalk racks of bright cottons called to him, the parade of colors inviting him to shop. Grandma had been pestering him to pick out materials for a quilt, something he chose himself, and with this fabric store in front of him, he might not be able to put her off any longer. Making a mental promise to buy the material when he had more time, he headed into Dennehy's general store for a few essentials.

"Daniel, wasn't it? Daniel Graham?" Mr. Dennehy stepped forward, his hand extended. "I was hoping you'd stop by. I wanted to thank you again for taking that fruit off my hands last week."

Danny fought down a moment's indecision about shaking the man's hand, his harsh treatment of Ben and Megan reason enough to maintain a distance, but he tried to balance instinct with lack of information. He may have walked in on the final act of a three-act play, and Mr. Dennehy might have good reason for overreacting.

"The Salvation Army food pantry in Wellsville put the fruit to good use." Danny shook the other man's hand and met his gaze squarely. "My grandmother is a firm believer in the 'do unto others' mind-set, and she's one smart cookie. We Grahams have learned not to cross her."

"Wisdom and age sometimes go hand in hand." Mr. Dennehy adopted an expression of concern that could have used more practice. A possible reason for that spoke up from behind the back counter.

"God helps those that help themselves!"

"Now, Mother..."

"Idle hands are the devil's workshop." The aged woman's voice harped on, her look tart and tight. "No one should go hungry in a land of opportunity like this one! Just plain lazy, if you ask me, that's what it is! Food shelf. Soup kitchens. Bah!"

"Mother, really..."

A woman breezed into the store, breaking a conversational thread Danny hadn't meant to start. She nodded to the proprietor, waved a hand of greeting to the grim-faced elderly woman behind the antique wooden counter, then raked Danny a look, stopped and sized him up. "You're new here."

How she guessed that instead of assuming he was a tourist, Danny had no idea. And wasn't sure he liked the assessment.

But her manner intrigued him. He angled his head, and offered his hand. "Daniel Graham."

She accepted the hand, but not without a slightly withering look. "You're staying with Megan Russo."

Her tone and choice of words made him want to jump to Megan's defense. He resisted. "I'm renting an apartment from Miss Russo while I'm in town on business, yes."

"That explains a lot." She sniffed displeasure, stepped back and moved to a rack of old-fashioned tins of cookies that held a shelf life of three years, minimal. Danny hated that kind of cookie. He wasn't even big on two-day-old cookies. He remembered the scent from Megan's kitchen, the heady aroma of chocolate chip as her friend rotated trays of big, round cookies onto tiered wire racks for cooling.

Every one of the cookies he'd consumed last night had turned his imaginings into reality. Megan Russo knew her way around an oven.

"Of course at Megan's age, a girl's got to be open to every possible opportunity that comes her way."

Tiny hairs of protest snaked a path up Danny's spine. His hands clenched. His jaw tightened.

The woman sent him an over-the-shoulder smirk as if privy to things he wasn't, rolled a shoulder of dismissal and turned back toward the grocer. "John, I need fresh fruit in the house for Brad Junior."

The grocer nodded, eager to switch to a more pleasant interchange. "I heard that Brad and his wife were coming to stay with you. Won't that be nice?

It's been a long time since you had a little boy running around your place, Jacqui."

"With all that's going on at our place, the last thing I need is a little boy running unleashed day in and day out, but it seems I had no choice in the matter. Megan had the only available apartment in the area and she rented it before I called last week."

So that was it.

Danny bit back a grin. Megan hadn't wanted to rent the apartment to him, that was painfully obvious in her reluctant attitude, the look of pain she'd bestowed on him as if he were the last-ditch effort she needed.

And all because she didn't want to rent the available space to an old boyfriend and his pregnant wife. He'd heard enough of her conversation with Hannah last week to realize how little fun there would have been in leasing the adjacent space to an old boyfriend and his family.

He bit back a smile, then turned when an exuberant voice belted out his name.

"Danny!"

"Ben. Hey." Danny moved across the store to the screened door and stepped outside. He grabbed Ben's hand and pumped it. "How you doin', man?"

"Good." Ben beamed, reached up and adjusted his Yankees baseball cap and gave a half shrug, still grinning. "Are you shopping?"

Danny was more scoping than shopping, but he nodded anyway. "Yes. How about you?"

Ben jerked a shoulder to the woman behind him. "Me and Mom had to do some—some—shopping."

"Excellent." Danny leaned around Ben to a woman who had to be Megan's mother, the resemblance a dead giveaway, and extended his hand. "I'm Danny Graham. I'm renting the apartment next to your daughter."

Megan's mother took his hand and offered an appreciative smile. "You're also the man who bought the fruit Ben toppled last week. I've been meaning to stop by and thank you for that. And I'm so glad you were able to rent the apartment. Meg is always guarding the bottom line, and having that space vacant was killing her."

"Respect for bottom-line efficiency is something she and I have in common," Danny noted. He indicated the unique mercantile with an angled gaze. "And I was actually able to put that fruit to good use. Accidents happen, right?"

"Inevitably. Although often with unexpected results." One look at her face made Danny realize that little got past Megan's mother. From the unhidden glint in her eye, he was pretty sure she saw right through him and his motives. Most of them, anyway.

"Things have a way of working out, don't they?" He sent her a grin, then noted Ben's hat with a pointed look. "You a real fan?"

"I love J-J-Jeter. He's my man!"

Danny grinned. Everyone loved Jeter, regardless of team affiliation. It was an unwritten rule of baseball because the Yankees captain epitomized sportsmanship. "You ever been to a game, Ben?"

"A—a Yankees game?"

"Yes."

Ben shook his head so hard a little spittle sprayed. Danny wiped the spot away without a second thought and casually ignored Mrs. Russo's look of concern.

"I've never been to—to—Yankee Stadium, but we see them on TV. Dad and Mom have cable."

Danny laughed out loud. "They do, huh? I might have to come over and catch some games because your sister isn't wired for cable yet. A fact I didn't know when I leased the apartment. I've already called and ordered it, though, because eight weeks with no baseball won't cut it."

Mrs. Russo frowned. "I can't believe she hasn't had that put in. Megan tends to take frugal to extremes. I'm glad you ordered it, Mr. Graham. It makes the rental more attractive to others in the long run. And do come over to the house and watch the games until they run cable to your apartment. We'd be honored to have you."

He met her smile and matched it. "I'd love to. They're playing at home Saturday night. Is that good for you guys? And what can I bring?"

"Just bring yourself," Megan's mother assured

him. "We've got plenty of snacks, and Megan's dad can grill hot dogs. Then we can pretend we're at the stadium."

"That's stellar seating right there," Danny agreed, grinning. "Thanks so much for the invite. I'll be there."

"And bring Meg, even if she tries to resist," her mother added before she resumed their walk. "She'll most likely have a list of things she thinks she needs to do with festival season upon us, but hopefully you can convince her otherwise."

Her smile said more than her words.

Pretty sure he'd found an ally, an important one at that, Danny nodded. "I'll do my best, ma'am."

Chapter Eight

Hannah entered the candy shop kitchen on Saturday morning and waved a slip of paper Meg's way. "A note for you."

"For me?"

Hannah raised her eyes skyward. "Your name's Megan, right?"

"I believe it is," Meg quipped back, her curiosity piqued. Caught at a critical moment in caramel making, Meg sent a look of frustration to Hannah. "Who's it from?"

Hannah held the note up to the light, scanned the contents, then grinned. "Cute guy next door."

"He signed it 'from the cute guy next door'?" Meg wondered out loud.

"No, he signed it 'Danny.' The embellishments were all me."

"What's it say?" Meg eyed the caramel mixture, decided it needed a minute more and hiked a brow, trying to stem her impatience. No luck.

"You can't wait 'til you're done with that and read it yourself?"

"No."

"Ah-hah." Hannah's smile suggested too much or maybe just enough, Meg wasn't sure, but she was totally certain she wanted to know what the note said sooner rather than later. "Hannah. Please?"

"Well, since you said please…" Hannah unfolded the note, added a ridiculous note of urgency to her voice and read, "Meg, your mother invited me to watch the Yankees game tonight. I'm supposed to bring you along. Since you've been avoiding me for forty-eight hours, I wanted to give you a heads-up before tonight to prepare any useless arguments you might throw my way. Feel free to wear appropriate Yankees fan apparel. Danny."

Meg went straight to the crux of the matter. "My mother invited him? Is that what that note says? Honestly?"

Hannah didn't try to hide her grin. "It does."

"On purpose?"

"So it would seem."

"I am so giving her a piece of my mind," Meg sputtered, striving to keep her attention on the boiling mixture while plotting and planning what to do with an interfering mother who should have known better. "What was she thinking?"

"Being nice?" Hannah suggested.

"No doubt that's what she'd want us to think." Meg scowled, tested the candy mix and frowned more deeply because it wasn't quite right yet and she needed both hands to throttle her mother.

"And isn't your mother working today?"

Hannah was right. The dental office in Wellsville was trying to accommodate people's crazy schedules and had started opening on Saturdays a few weeks back. Her mother alternated Saturdays with the other hygienist, and today was her day to work.

"You can yell at her later, though," Hannah added, teasing. "Because why on Earth would you want to spend Saturday night with a cute guy, eating hot dogs and watching baseball on a big-screen TV?"

"Cute guy?" Alyssa Michaels walked in the back door, breathed deep and sighed in delight at the combined scents of cookies and candy. "Meg's giving the guy next door a chance? Tell me more."

Hannah hooked a thumb toward the van outside. "I would, but we've got a booth at the strawberry festival, and I promised I'd deliver the cookies to the girls staffing it."

Meg studied the drizzle of caramel, nodded satisfaction, switched the burner off and moved the big, cast-aluminum pot to the table behind her. "Are you sure you're okay doing the ice cream stand with Crystal tonight? After dropping this stuff off and working at the library?"

"Positive." Hannah's matter-of-fact voice said it wasn't a big deal, but Meg knew it made for a long day. "The library is only open for six hours, and it's the last Saturday until after Labor Day, so it's fine,

Meg. And the extra money I make here over the summer makes a big difference in my finances."

"And having Hannah help Crystal tonight means you're free to watch baseball with the cute guy," Alyssa added.

"Except that I planned on getting ahead for tomorrow." Megan poured caramel into the molds carefully. The intoxicating mix of dark sugar and milk chocolate delighted her senses while her mind thought of her mother's possible motives for extending an invitation to Danny. Karen Russo knew better. She'd witnessed Meg's heartbreak, her embarrassment. Both times. What was she thinking?

Determined, Meg turned her attention back to the task at hand. The work she did now made up for the lack of business midwinter, and as busy as summer was for a store owner and festival vendor, Meg would have plenty of time to rest come January, February and March. Those three months could make or break a business in this climate, and while Meg might be a little soft in matters of the heart, she was tough in the ways of the business world. Covering her bottom line meant work now, play later.

"You ready, Megs? It's six-fifteen. Game time is seven-oh-five."

Megan turned toward Danny's voice, scanned his worn Major League Baseball T-shirt, and shook her head as she set out fudge pans. "Working. Sorry. Enjoy yourself, though."

Danny stepped in, eyed the cold stove and grabbed her hand. "There's a game on, Miss Russo. Time to go."

She frowned, wishing the feel of his fingers didn't warm her somewhere in the vicinity of her heart. Their meshed fingers felt just right.

"Yankees versus Tampa Bay," he urged, imploring, tugging her toward the door, his smile cute and possibly lethal. "You got my note, right? We're watching it at your parents' house."

"*We're* doing no such thing," she corrected smoothly. She pulled her hand free, turned and rolled her right shoulder, trying to ease a persistent kink.

"Sore?" Danny moved behind her and pressed the flat of his hand between her shoulder blade and the center of her back.

"Ouch. Yes. Right…"

"Here." Danny indicated the area with the flat of his hand and then kneaded the muscle below with gentle fingers. "You've got a knot here from using your right arm continuously."

"I'm right-handed, thereby limiting my options."

"Push yourself to alternate hands," he advised, his hands working some kind of delightful magic against the taut muscle that stretched from midback to her shoulder. "Your trapezius is taking a beating on this side."

Or she could just have him massage the fatigue away each night. The appeal of that made her step away. "Thanks. It's fine. And how did you wrangle an invite to my parents' house out of the blue like this?"

"It's we, not I, and your mother took pity on me because I didn't have cable. And you have Hannah and Crystal running the ice cream stand all evening. I know. I checked."

"I have work to do."

"All work and no play—"

"Says the guy who disappears at first light and stays gone all day." He flinched a little, just enough to make Meg wonder about his purpose in town. "Rumor has it you're secretly a federal agent, working on some big case hidden in the Appalachian foothills."

"That comes off as way more exciting than the reality." He jerked his head toward her side of the house. "Do you need a jacket? A sweater?"

"No, because I'm not going."

He didn't move, just stood silent, watching. Waiting. The warm look of gentle expectation had her rethinking every horrible thing she'd ever said about men the past four years. His eyes, calm and steady, said he'd wait her out. The tiny grin that quirked his mouth meant he had the patience to do just that. And she hadn't hung out with Ben in days…

"All right."

His grin deepened.

"But not because you're pressuring me," she scolded. She called goodbye to Hannah and Crystal, patently ignoring Hannah's profile smile. "I haven't had time to do anything with Ben all week."

"And there's nothing like a Saturday night baseball game to offer bonding opportunities," Danny finished for her. "Exactly my point. And your father's cooking hot dogs."

"This just gets better and better, doesn't it?"

She started to turn away as they rounded the corner of the house, but Danny caught her arm.

"Hey."

She kept her gaze down, feeling trapped by the combination of Danny, her parents' invitation, Ben's behavior problems...

He raised her chin and met her gaze. "They're just being friendly because I bought the fruit last week."

"The..." She hesitated, puzzled, not expecting this turn of events. "What?"

"The fruit Ben knocked over," Danny explained. "I bought it. John Dennehy told your mother what I'd done and when she saw me in town, she invited me. Nothing more, nothing less. No one is setting you up. Least of all your mother."

Megan sighed. She turned her gaze away from him and focused on a spot over his shoulder, then worked her jaw and blew out a breath. "All right. I'm sorry."

"For?"

She met his eyes, deciding they were way too gorgeous to be ignored. "Thinking it was something else. Jumping to conclusions that had no base in reality."

"What if they have a base in reality? What then?"

"But they don't." She countered his words by striding forward, refusing to meet his gaze, her focus undivided. "So it's not an issue."

"It could be an issue. If we let it."

The look of frustration returned, but not nearly as dark or deep. "No. It couldn't."

"You sure?"

"Listen, I—" She turned, peeved that he refused to drop the topic, irritated by the opportunity he offered and the fact that it tempted her at all.

His grin disarmed her. She stood stock-still on the sidewalk, looking up at him, the glint in his eye, the strength of his squared jaw, the strong set of his shoulders even in a faded Yankees T-shirt that had seen better days.

Part of her wanted to melt.

Part of her wanted to smack him for being so nice, so inviting, so comfortable with himself, his teasing words tugging her back into a game she'd been burned at twice. Where was her resolve? Her backbone? She couldn't trust herself, her judgment, her choices, not when it came to matters of the heart. She'd proven that in front of the whole town.

Danny stepped closer, a part of him wanting nothing more than to wipe the frown from her face, erase the tiny lines of worry etched by a pair of jerks who didn't know a good thing when they saw it, then realized he was probably no better. His plans didn't include the happy ending girls sought, although something about Megan made that seem almost possible.

But it wasn't. And he knew that, and still he moved forward, letting his gaze search her eyes, her face, her mouth…

A gentle brush of the lips, that was all he intended. Just a hint of her, the delightful mix of old and new that was Megan Russo, a fellow entrepreneur and candy maker, a young woman whose spirit called out to him despite all the reasons this couldn't possibly work.

She smelled of vanilla and chocolate with a hint of toasted almond, a heady combination that drew him, a mix of familiarity and something else, something uniquely Megan, an allure that had called to him every time he deliberately passed her door without a look, without a glance, chin down until he got to his car. And then he managed to stay gone all day, until after the ice cream window closed at nine-thirty, making himself scarce until she was safely tucked in her apartment. Out of sight.

Not out of mind.

"Danny."

He paused the kiss, wondering if she felt the same way, wondering if simple proximity sent her heart into a danger zone the way his had done, half hoping it had, almost afraid it didn't.

He stepped back, knowing too much, who he was and why he was there in Allegany County, looking to develop a store close enough to threaten her business.

She started to speak, but he shushed her with a gentle finger to her mouth. "One day at a time. Please."

She shook her head, but her eyes said something different, a tiny spark of hope brightening the gold flecks. "Danny, I—"

"Don't want to be hurt, used or embarrassed in front of the entire town again," he filled in for her. "I get that. What I don't get is—" he waved his free hand between them, indicating her, then himself "—this. But I can't deny it, either, and I've spent most of the past week skulking in and out so I didn't see you, couldn't hear you and wouldn't be tempted to stop by and make you smile. See you laugh." He brushed a hand across her forehead, smoothing tiny wisps of curl back away from her face. "But I can't spend the next seven weeks doing that. So either I move out and find a place that doesn't have your smile, your cute old-fashioned dresses that make me appreciate American history in a way old Mr. Gorham never could in high school…"

Her smile deepened, the dimple on her left cheek flashing just for him.

"Or I stay in my apartment and we stop pretending that we're not listening for one another. Or sneaking peeks out the window."

She blushed.

He grinned.

"And since it goes both ways, I suggest we see where it leads us."

Megan stepped back, reality urging caution. "In less than two months it's going to take you away. Whereas I'm going to be right here, stirring chocolate, molding candies and dishing up ice cream treats for the football teams after practices."

"Possibly. But how will we know if we don't take a chance?"

"Well, Danny, I've taken chances." Megan took a broader step away. "And I'm not so big on them right now. You've been in town long enough to know that I've been the object of discussion, and you overheard enough last week to explain why, so it's probably best if we just maintain a nice, friendly business relationship. End of story."

She refused to dwell on that kiss. How she got lost in the moment, totally dazzled, as if her heart and soul were there for the taking. That in itself was reason to run. She couldn't afford any more stupid mistakes. A girl's heart could take only so much. Right?

His expression said she hadn't exactly convinced him. Oh, well. She'd convinced herself, and that was all she needed right now.

He took her hand.

"Danny."

"Stop."

She stopped. Breathed. Glanced up.

He didn't look amused. Or teasing. He looked downright, gut-wrenchingly sincere. He glanced down to their joined hands. "This just feels right. Doesn't it?"

The fact that it did only scared her more.

"Megan?"

She bit her lip and glanced down before bringing her gaze back up to his. "Yes?"

"Trust me."

She winced inside, then dropped his hand. "Wrong words, Danny." She continued walking through the village, the early evening sounds of kids at play and summer birds a wonderful combination of old-school, small-town warmth.

He followed, hands thrust in his pockets. She glanced back and saw his face, read his look and tried to smother the feeling of anticipation his expression inspired. Despite his humor, his teasing, his easygoing nature, she suspected Danny Graham generally got what he wanted, when he wanted it.

But she was off-limits.

Sure you are, an inner voice scoffed. *You totally melted into that kiss. You think he couldn't tell that?*

Another glance back said she hadn't fooled him a bit. It was there in his measured walk, his quiet appraisal, his "she'll come back to me if I give her time" magnetism.

Megan shrugged it all off. She was beyond the

magnetic phase of romance. Totally. As long as she didn't gaze at him too much. See that smile. Meet those eyes. Remember that kiss.

But she couldn't help remembering it, and that didn't bode well. Not well at all.

"Danny! You came over!" Ben charged forth as soon as they turned up the paved driveway of the house, his happiness unabashed. Danny grinned back, glad that Ben was openly happy to see him, and wondering what he was thinking to corner Meg like that.

Except he'd do it again in a heartbeat if he had the chance.

But after seeing the vulnerability in her face, her eyes, he couldn't take a chance on playing her for a fool. Not knowing the full truth about him wasn't right. He should tell her who he was, let things fall where they may. But she might hate him.

Correction: *Of course* she'd hate him. She was a businesswoman, right down to the toes. He admired that about her, her willingness to do whatever it took to maintain a strong business in the face of a tough economy. Few people had that stamina.

Megan did.

And he stood poised to take it all away from her because, as cute as her store was, brand names like Grandma Mary's held them in good stead throughout the Northeast and mid-Atlantic states.

Danny swallowed a sigh and reached out a hand to Ben. "Are we ready for a win?"

"Y-yes! A-Rod is bustin' loose and Jeter's the—the—man!"

"You've got that right."

"Danny?"

Danny reached out to shake the hand of an older man, tall, broad and in his midfifties. "Mr. Russo?"

"Adam, please. You got her to come?" Megan's father leaned his head in Megan's direction, a brow shifted up.

"Under duress, but, yes, although we nearly lost out to fudge preparation."

Adam shot him a quick look. "Employing diversionary tactics, is she?"

Danny grinned. "Yes, sir."

"And you counterattacked?"

"Played the guilt card, sir."

"You realize that she's surrounded herself with an invisible force field?"

"I've been bounced off once or twice. Obviously a slow learner, sir."

Adam's look of amusement softened a hair. "And you understand the shield was created out of necessity, right?"

"Duly noted. Is this where you threaten me bodily harm if I break her heart?"

Adam sent him a look that wasn't close to amused. "She's had enough of those. Partially her fault, but mostly not. She's totally up front and honest. And sometimes that's been her undoing. I'd really like someone who appreciates those qualities. A refreshing change, if you get my drift."

Oh, Danny got it all right. And then some. Add her father to the list of people who would outright hate him when they realized who he was. What he was doing there.

"Danny! The game's on!" Ben lumbered their way, his warm smile a welcome mat. "Mom's got more f-food in the kitchen."

"Well, let's go, big guy." He nodded to Adam. "You need help bringing those in, sir?"

Adam shook his head. "I've got 'em, thanks. And you've got a big admirer in my boy here. Ben loves having another Yankees fan around."

"I see that. And since your sister was too frugal to put in cable before this…" He shot a glance to Meg to see if she was listening. Her rolled eyes confirmed that for him. "…I won't have it for five more days. That's the entire Tampa Bay series and half the Boston games."

"Well, feel free to come by and watch them here," Megan's mother offered, as they entered the kitchen through a back door. "Ben and Adam love a good game. The more the merrier."

Megan shot her mother a "what are you thinking" look that Danny intercepted. He grinned at her purposely. "I love homes with open-door policies. My parents are like that, too. Everyone's welcome. Just one big, happy family."

Meg huffed. He smiled, knowing he shouldn't tease her, but totally unable to resist a little fun at her expense. "So far I'm holding my own with your parents and your brother, Megs. Three out of four." He nodded toward the big-screen TV. "In baseball terms, I'm batting seven-fifty. Pretty solid."

She kept her gaze trained on a perfectly grilled hot dog. "If I was coaching you'd be on the first bus back to Scranton, rookie. Minor leagues, all the way. Way too predictable for big-league pitching."

He laughed and filled his plate, an odd feeling stealing over him. A feeling of belonging. Of coming home. Which was ridiculous since he had a nice home.

Well, his parents had a nice home. He hadn't settled into anything other than rentals in a lot of years. His own fault, he knew, but in his busy life, renting here or there became a convenience, business suites hotels becoming his home away from home.

Until now.

Here in Jamison he was caught in the fabric of small-town living, a lifestyle he thought he'd deplore as a younger man. Wrong. The peace and quiet called to him, the winding roads, wooded hills and sprawling farms. The wide ribbon of the Genesee River cut a swath through Wellsville, traveling north to Lake Ontario, a beautiful waterway fed by creeks and streams.

Meg sent him a look, curious and cautious. He knew he had to come clean about who he was, why he was here, but for the life of him he didn't want to have this end before seeing where it could lead.

Selfish?

No, he decided as he crossed the room to her, smiling. Where Meg was concerned, he didn't think he had a selfish bone in his body.

He fit in, Meg decided midgame, when the left fielder was caught stealing second on an obviously bad call by the second-base umpire.

Danny surged to his feet alongside her father and brother, lamenting the ref's lack of prescription eye-wear in a loud voice, and when the replay confirmed their collective decision, the three men groaned in unison before discussing the use of video review until Meg was tempted to stifle them all.

Instead, she hit the volume button until the play-by-play grew loud enough to make her point. "I paid to hear the announcers, not you guys."

"Feisty." Danny grinned, moved over to settle in alongside her, and pretended to be on his best behavior. "But cute."

"And you didn't pay a thing," her father reminded her, one brow thrust up. "Which is why Danny's here instead of in his own living room, feet up, eating a pizza."

"This is much better, sir." Danny met Adam's gaze with a smile and swept the broad family room with a look of appreciation. "All the comforts of home, a great TV, wonderful company and a beautiful woman."

Adam's grin said Danny made the short list.

Megan refused to entertain such notions. The only lists she was interested in right now involved cookie and fudge production for festival booths. Keeping her store stocked. The summer loomed long and frantically busy, the quick rotation of town festivals a big part of her bottom line, and Meg took those numbers seriously.

Danny's self-confidence and quick wit called to her, but the reality of his life meant he'd be leaving, so why would she test the waters? Her home was here, her life, her family, her work...

Danny leaned closer, his gaze on the television, his words for her ears only. "Remember that mustard seed, Megs?"

"My name is Megan."

He grinned, still facing forward. "Sometimes things grow from tiny bits of faith, tiny seeds of life."

"Danny Graham, philosopher."

He shrugged, still watching the game, then shifted a glance her way, a quick look, his expression warm and teasing. "Thanks for coming with me."

She wanted to growl something back, something that made him realize she wasn't a bit interested, but she couldn't. Instead she slanted him a smile that made his eyes brighten, his smile deepen. "I'm glad I did." She nodded toward the television and tucked her feet beneath her, feeling totally relaxed for the first time in months, not caring if it was Danny or the game or the situation, just feeling…good.

She settled in, hugging a Yankees couch pillow and decided it was time to relax and enjoy the game. A big part of her hoped she was just talking baseball, but a hint of conscience probed the bigger picture and sighed within.

Here we go again.

Chapter Nine

The melodic strains of "The Candy Man" woke Danny early the next morning. He scowled at the clock that read eight-ten, remembered it was Sunday, then groped for the phone, his mother's ringtone in keeping with the family theme. He hauled the phone to his ear. "Don't you have clocks in Buffalo?"

"We do and they're working fine," she shot back. "Good morning, Daniel. How's everything going?"

He should have called and checked in. By not calling he'd aroused her curiosity, because he always checked in while scouting business locations and deals. They made a good team, his parents and him. And Grandma, of course, although she wasn't as involved in the day-to-day as she had been. That thought niggled him. He hadn't stopped back at the quilt store yet. Maybe he could do that today. He yawned, stretched and focused on his mother's question. "Good. Mostly."

"Ah-hah."

"Nothing bad," he assured her. "I'm just trying to weigh possible sites and come out on top with as few people hating us as possible."

"Why would anyone hate us? Hate chocolate? Hate candy? An impossibility."

"Not candy in general. There's an old-fashioned chocolate shop here in Jamison and I'm trying to be careful so we don't drive her out of business."

"Is she in a good location?"

Danny mulled that. "Yes and no. She's got better proximity to the interstate, but she's in a tiny town that's purposely caught in a time machine. They get a good tourist draw for six months of the year. And then there's Thanksgiving and Christmas, but we'll probably take a chunk of that business away if I buy the storefront I'm eyeing in Wellsville."

"Survival of the fittest, Daniel."

"Well…" He hesitated, picking his words. "It's not that easy."

"Why?"

"Because she's…nice. Sweet. And she's developed this business from the bottom up, so I don't want to mess it up for her."

"Danny, I appreciate your thoughtfulness, probably more than most, but I don't see how putting a small tribute store for Grandma Mary's in Wellsville will have a huge effect on some little old lady's shop up Route 19," his mother argued. "And aren't you the one always spewing numbers back at me? You thought this area wouldn't support a candy shop at all—now you see it's supporting one that's in a less than perfect location. So what's the problem?"

"She's not old."

"Oh?" A slight pause ensued. "Oh."

Danny ignored her. "And this area is beginning to resurge, so we might be able to capitalize on that. That's lessened my concerns considerably."

"O-kay." His mother drew the two syllables out slowly. "So, once more. What's the holdup?"

He absolutely refused to say too much. "I'm trying to strike a balance. An important balance. Let's leave it at that for the moment."

She was silent for long, slow ticks of the clock, weighing his words as if trying to decipher this change of attitude. "All right. You'll let Dad or me know if you need help, right?"

He laughed. "I sincerely do not need help. But I do need my balloon. Can you have it brought down here in a few weeks? Wellsville has a big balloon rally in mid-July. I want to have a little fun before I make everyone mad at me."

"Mad at you…"

Oops, he'd said too much. "Mom, you know how it goes. We're the big guns, swooping into town to take out the little guy."

"Danny, it's a candy store, not a Super Wal-Mart. For pity's sake, get a grip. And go to church. They must have a church in that little town, right?"

They had five. He'd discovered just how cute that was last Sunday morning. Five churches, all with bell towers, pealing their calls to worship alternately.

No one was allowed to sleep in on Sunday mornings. Not in Jamison.

He laughed. "You would be quite comfortable with the church-to-population ratio. And you never know. I just might."

She laughed, smug. "I knew sending you down there would be good for you. A chance to reconnect with your roots."

"My roots are in Williamsville, remember?"

"Ancestral roots, boy. And don't be a smart aleck. There's a lot to be learned in a small town. And this has given your sister a chance to spread her wings. Get back in the game."

"Have you talked with her?"

A more plaintive note colored her tone. "Yes. And she's doing fine."

"But it's hard," Danny added.

His mother hesitated. He could picture her in the big country kitchen in Williamsville, her forehead knit, a pencil tapping against the counter or the table, an old habit that refused to die. "It is," she finally agreed. "Which makes it all the more necessary."

"If she needs help, I can be just about anywhere in a few hours' time," Danny reminded her. "There's only an airstrip here, but I could fly out of Rochester or Buffalo. Or drive."

"I know you could. Dad said the same thing, but then it looks like we don't trust her to do the job, and that's a risk I can't take. Not when she's this fragile."

"But is she *too* fragile?" Danny asked, concern edging his voice.

"No." Merrilee Romesser's reply took a firm turn. "And we've got to be careful not to expect too much, too soon. It's only been a couple of weeks with you down there and Mary Clare stepping into your shoes, so we'll just give it time."

A part of Danny longed to swoop in and grab his sister and cocoon her until the loss of her fiancé didn't cut as deep, but his mother had already taken a stand with both Romesser men to let Mary Clare spread her wings. Take a chance, a leap of faith. Tucked away in sweet, bucolic Jamison, it was hard to do. "We could still switch spots."

"No." His mother's voice said that wasn't about to happen. "It's good for her to jump into the mainstream and it's good for you to take a breath, Daniel. Smell a flower. Go to a small-town festival with a pretty girl."

Visions of Meg filled him, the sweet, old-world dresses, the colloquial turns of speech, the lacy hairnet she wore on occasion. Then and there he decided his mother was absolutely right. He wanted to stay here for the summer, get the tribute store up and running, and get to know his neighbor. But if his sister needed help… "You'll let me know if you need me, though, right? I'm enjoying this assignment, but if Mary Clare gets into trouble—"

"I'll let you know," his mother interrupted.

Danny stood, rolled his shoulders, then filled the glass coffee carafe, yawning. "Gotta go. The church service starts in an hour."

"You're actually going?" His mother's surprise made him laugh.

"I think I will. You can't sleep through the church bells around here anyway, so why not? Talk to you later this week."

"Okay."

He glanced at the clock again. He had just enough time to get cleaned up and ready if Megs was true to form. She'd left the house for church at nine-ten the previous week. If he just happened to be walking in the same direction for a similar purpose, well…

Timing was everything, right?

> Danny Graham.

The guy was haunting her in a most annoying fashion. She thought about him when he wasn't around, and when he was.

And now he'd gone and kissed her, which incited a whole new round of thoughts.

And feelings. Amazing feelings.

She shut them down with a firm grasp on reality. Her beautifully planned autumn wedding the previous year had morphed into a town gossipfest. Not exactly the fairy-tale ending she'd sought.

Fairy tales were fictional for a reason. She remembered that as she slipped into a pink floral dress. She'd play the historic candy maker later that day, but for church she was just another modern-day girl meeting the family at weekly services. And if Danny Graham happened to notice, well…

What had he said about peeking through windows, watching for each other? She'd blushed at the realization, and then doused a spark of hope inspired by his admission that he'd been watching, too.

If he was watching this morning, she wanted to look good. A quick glance in the mirror said she'd managed that. She smiled and headed out the door, only to run into the man himself.

"Nice." His gaze swept down, then up, his look appreciative. "Very nice. It appears you have no trouble with twenty-first-century garb, Megs."

"My name is Megan."

"I know. Are those shoes okay to walk in?"

"I was thinking of driving this morning." It wasn't exactly a lie. The thought popped into her head when she walked out the door and found Danny waiting for her. "Would you like a ride?"

"Let's walk." He held out his arm.

She ignored it and shrugged. "Plenty of time, I suppose."

"And a beautiful morning."

"It is."

He thrust his hands into his pockets and strolled

alongside her, quiet and comfortable, as if he wasn't making her heart beat a mile a minute at the thought of being seen together, walking through town on a Sunday morning.

Oh, the gossips would be wagging their tongues. Shaking their heads. Wringing their hands at her expense.

Danny leaned her way. "We're just two people walking to church together. Nothing to get all steamed up over."

She sent him a sidelong glance. "You've never lived in a small town, have you?"

"Not a rural small town, no. But a suburban one."

"Population?"

He pondered that and nodded. "I see your point. Our high school classes had over four hundred kids."

"Eighty-nine."

"Big difference, yes, but—"

"There are no buts. You can't argue facts and figures. Not only am I 'small town,' we're tucked in a region that's been knocked around a lot the past twenty years. We've got an aging population, little growth influx and our kids are moving away in record numbers."

"But not you," he argued. "And those facts are starting to change, right? Isn't Walker Electronics expanding?"

He was right. Alyssa's husband, Trent, had returned to Jamison to work for Walker Electronics the year before, to help the town. And it was working, but...

"It's a long process," she told him. "It doesn't happen overnight."

"Most things don't, Megs."

"Megan."

He grinned. Winked.

And suddenly she started thinking Megs was about the cutest name she ever heard. But no way was she about to let him know it. Confident, smug, overbearing...

He clasped her hand, the touch gentle. Warm. Firm. She started to back off and he swung their joined hands forward, his gaze down. "They're happier like this, Megs. Don't you think?"

He was ridiculous. Endearing. Nice. And he'd gotten up early to walk her to church.

What are you doing? her inner voice demanded. *What are you thinking? Haven't you had enough? This is a recipe for disaster. Walk away now while you still have a shred of dignity.*

She should listen to herself. She really should. But having her hand in Danny's felt good. No, it felt wonderful. And the look he sidled her, a teasing look that made her want to laugh out loud, no words necessary, enticed her to take a chance.

She hadn't laughed a lot these past nine months. She'd worked, prayed, waited and done her share of whining. It felt good to laugh. Especially good to laugh with a man again.

Which would be her downfall, no doubt. "You understand the predicament you're putting me in, right?"

He nodded. Squeezed her hand. "Oh, I get it. Life's a risk. I think we all find that out the hard way."

"Did you?"

"Don't we all? Hey, if the quilt shop is open on Sundays, can we stop in after church? I need to buy something for my grandmother."

Something for his grandmother? The sweetness of that almost turned Meg's insides to mush. Almost. "Main Street does a lot of Sunday tourist business, and Maude McGinnity is one sharp businesswoman. She'll be open by the time the service ends."

"Perfect. One more thing I can check off my list."

"And that list includes…?" Meg left the question open-ended.

Danny shrugged but looked less than comfortable. "Too many things to ponder on a beautiful Sunday morning. Are we sitting with your parents?"

Megan sighed out loud.

Danny grinned.

"They like you. Ben likes you. The dog even likes you, but he doesn't count because he likes every-one."

"Should I be insulted?"

"Possibly. But while I like you, too, I'm not in any way, shape or form inclined to be involved at this stage of the game."

"You are holding my hand," he reminded her.

Oh, she knew that. Right down to her pretty little hot-pink painted toenails, the warmth of those clasped fingers making her think things she'd thought before. Twice before, as a matter of fact.

She was an admitted romantic. Who else would dress in period costume to cook and teach people about days gone by?

But pragmatism took over when she'd waited long, drawn-out minutes at Good Shepherd church, the corset-laced wedding dress tight and heavy as time dragged on, her apprehension building, as she realized her groom would never show up.

She'd been able to rationalize Brad's treatment of her after a while. Obviously Denise had been willing to do things she'd refused before their wedding, hence their preschool-aged son, born five months after the wedding.

But Michael…

She'd believed him. Trusted. And yeah, if she was honest, she should have realized it wasn't a perfect relationship. He'd let things slide she'd never be careless with, he wasn't diligent to detail, and he wasn't exactly Mr. Ambitious.

But he'd been sweet, kind and funny. Very funny. And obviously humor was one of her downfalls because here she was, walking hand in hand with

Danny, admiring his quick smile, his beautiful eyes and quick wit.

Time to draw the line in the sand.

She wriggled her hand free, tilted her head and angled him a scolding look. "As much fun as this is," she acknowledged, sweeping their hands a quick glance before raising her gaze to his, "I'm putting the brakes on."

"Because?"

"The whole summer love thing? It only works for teenagers on vacation. Not me, not here, not now. End of discussion. We're neighbors. Maybe friends, given enough time. But that's it." She paused, firmed her gaze and met his look of invitation frankly. "I've got my busy season upon me, tourists left and right, a candy-making schedule that keeps me up at night and an ice cream business that makes me just enough extra income now to offset the slower months of winter. I can't afford to mess things up by chasing rainbows."

Danny's grin said he'd just scored a point. "Chasing Rainbows is the name of my balloon."

She paused as they approached the church steps. "Your what?"

He reached forward and brushed a stray lock of hair from her face, tucking the errant curl behind her ear.

"My hot air balloon. I'm using it in the Wellsville rally. My grandfather named the first one nearly fifty years back. We've been piloting a rainbow-themed balloon ever since."

"You're a pilot?"

"Yes." He stepped closer, ignoring the people arriving around them, his gaze trained on Megan alone. "Would you ride with me? I'd love to take you up. Show you the hills from above. The trees, the towns, the farmers' fields. It's all different from the basket of a balloon."

"No."

He paused her entrance into the church with a hand to her arm. The feel of his hand, strong and sure against the soft skin of her upper arm, took her places she'd decided to avoid.

She stepped away from his touch, saw him note that, the arched brow and steady gaze missing little. "You're not scared, are you?"

"No."

He tilted his head.

Drat. She'd said it too quick.

"You are." He didn't step forward, just leaned in, invading her space, smelling of fresh, spiced aftershave, his scent enveloping her. "I'll keep you safe."

As with his trust request from the previous night, Megan wasn't buying it. Lofting skyward in one of those gorgeous balloons with a heartthrob like Danny who was already ruining her decisions to avoid men at all costs?

"I'm a terra-firma-type gal. Both feet planted on the ground."

"Ballooning offers a whole new vantage point, Megs."

Her vantage point of avoiding heartbreak was just fine, thank you very much. She sent him a smile she hoped wasn't quite as acid as it felt and headed into the church. "No, thanks."

Chapter Ten

Danny could have pushed his point and sat with Meg during the service, but he excelled at corporate deal making for a reason. He knew when to back off and when to press. Right now, she needed thinking time. And was he terrible for equating Megan with one of his business deals?

That was how he saw things. Black and white. Bottom lines. His job demanded attention to detail. So did romance. Although he wasn't looking for romance.

One glance across the crowded small church nixed that notion. He might not have been looking, but it seemed to have found him. Now what to do about it?

He wasn't accustomed to being caught in the middle, and didn't like the feeling. Megan was the sweetest thing he'd ever laid eyes on.

And beneath her tough exterior laid the heart of a gentle woman. Understandable, considering her romantic past. But scaling those walls would be no easy task. And she was right, in any case.

He'd be gone midsummer. Oh, sure, he'd come back to oversee the new store's setup and hire staff. He'd get it up and running, but regardless of how well Mary Clare handled her projects along the East Coast, he'd have work-related travel obligations during the busy fall and holiday seasons.

He loved big cities, the hustle and bustle, the mayhem. But sitting in the whitewashed church where the combination of beeswax candles and old wood offered quiet reprieve, something inside wound down, just a touch. He'd grown careless in his wanderings, and regular church attendance had fallen along the wayside, but this…

He let the soft hum of whispered conversation embrace him, the yellow glow of antique lighting very Currier and Ives, a glimpse of yesteryear. Surprisingly, he liked it, but then he'd found little *not* to like in Jamison, and that was due in no small part to the lovely young woman who sat eight pews up.

An older man nudged his arm and motioned left. "The missus needs a music book."

"Oh. Of course." Danny reached behind him, procured the book, then grabbed another for the man. He held out both.

The man accepted one and shrugged off the second. "We'll share. Church ain't got quite enough to go 'round in the summer when folks visit, so we're used to it, and she knows ever' one of them hymns by heart so it ain't like she even needs the thing, but she feels better havin' it in hand." He nodded to the remaining book, his wizened look steadfast. "You can have that one."

Danny met the old man's gaze, the wisdom of years gone by a soft sheen of faded blue. He nodded, smiled, then realized he truly meant the smile, and that realization made him feel better yet.

Megan waited deliberately to see Reverend Hannity, sure that Danny would have trekked home by the time she exited the church long minutes later.

Nope.

And he didn't even have the decency to pretend he wasn't waiting for her, to act as if his presence was circumstantial. He stood poised on the sidewalk, one hand on the railing, one foot propped on the step above, gazing up, and then he had the nerve to grace her with that heart-stopping grin the minute she stepped out the door. As she descended the steps he released the rail and straightened. "You were hoping I'd be gone."

"And yet, you aren't."

"The quilt store, remember?" He indicated the Quiltin' Bee with a casual wave of his hand. "You agreed to stop in with me."

"I agreed to no such thing." Face forward, she willed herself not to chance a glance his way. His humor and charm were eroding her concerns, putting her in a precarious position, and she'd had enough of those to last a lifetime.

"What if I sweeten the deal with a maple twist from Seb Walker's store?"

Danny Graham didn't play fair. Seb Walker carried melt-in-your-mouth Amish pastries with seasonal fruit or layered custards.

"Or a fry pie?"

"Your pick, my lady."

She turned toward the pastry window, but Danny redirected her toward Maude's. "Not so fast. No way am I looking through materials with sticky hands. Quilt shop first."

He made a good point. Maude McGinnity was a Jamison cornerstone, a descendant of one of Jamison's original nineteenth-century settlers and related to a fair share of the county. Maude took great pride in her store. She glanced up as they entered, and gave a firm nod. "Good morning, Megan. And…?"

Danny stepped forward, his hand out, obviously comfortable, a skill that said selling himself came easily, a quality Meg found intimidating. "Daniel Graham. Nice to meet you. And you are…?"

"Maude McGinnity. Graham." Maude tested the name thoughtfully, eyeing him as if finding something askew. He gave her a straight-on grin, reminding Meg he had no trouble charming people.

"Do you have family here?" Maude asked, her gaze curious.

Danny shook his head. "I'm here on business, but I've been promising my grandmother I'd send her material for a quilt, so your shop is perfect."

Maude's expression said she'd like to know more, but she wasn't one to pry.

Danny turned toward Meg. "You're good at all this old-fashioned stuff, Megs. What do you think?"

"Megs?" Maude's quick uptake shooed Megan toward the wall of fabrics.

"Obviously misspoken," Meg assured Maude, offering Danny the better part of her back as she moved farther into the store. No way in this world was she about to offer more fodder for the gossip mill.

"Your grandmother likes quilts?" Maude swung back toward Danny and indicated the racks of hanging quilts mounted along the side walls. "We've got all different types here, from hand-done Amish to country colonial."

"Actually Grandma quilts beautifully," Danny explained. He waved a hand toward the stunning array of hand-stitched blankets lining the front room of the shop. "She's like an artist with calico."

"Really?" Maude's look sharpened. "Does she live around here?"

"Not anymore."

"But she did," Maude's tone mused.

Danny shrugged and looked a little uncomfortable, just enough to make Meg wonder why that might be a sore spot.

He worked his jaw, conceding. "A long time ago. When she was a girl. The family's been in the Buffalo area for two generations now."

"And no family hereabouts?"

"Not that I know of."

"Hmm…"

"Like I said…" A hint of relief brightened Danny's eyes, making Meg wonder why having family here would be an issue. "It was a long time ago."

"When you're looking at seventy-five, you get to know a lot of folks," Maude shot back. "But no Grahams come to mind."

Danny moved left, effectively changing the subject by withdrawing a bolt of material. "This blue print's nice, isn't it?"

"Beautiful." A tiny smile softened Maude's mouth as she stroked a finger across the smooth, clean cotton. "And if you coupled it with that gingham, you'd have a nice effect."

"And this solid." Megan held up a bolt in the slightly darker periwinkle of the tiniest flower in the shaded blue calico. "It brings out the depth of the flowers without drawing too much attention to itself."

"And this green draws out the stems and the leaves," Maude noted.

Danny gave her a quick nod. "Can you cut me enough for a quilt top?"

Maude's mouth pursed in puzzlement. "It's hard to figure yardage without knowing what pattern she might choose. A good quilt top is all about balance." She stepped to the back room and motioned Danny to follow her. "I have three Amish women who quilt on weekday afternoons. This is some of their current handiwork."

Danny whistled low, the stretched quilt a work of art.

"But each pattern requires specific amounts. And the size of a quilt makes a difference, too. What would this be used for?"

Danny flicked a teasing glance Meg's way. "According to my grandmother, it's for my marriage bed."

Meg choked.

Maude grinned, a hand covering her mouth, her self-control waning as seconds ticked by.

Danny held his hands aloft, palms out. "It's her idea, not mine, but she's been after me for years."

"For the material or a wife?"

Maude's query made him laugh. "Both. But we'll settle for material today. It will make her happy and I'd do anything to make my grandma happy. I can ship it off to her tomorrow."

"Queen-size bed?"

Danny drew himself taller, grinning. "King-size."

"Oh, brother," Megan quipped.

"Oh, my." Maude giggled outright, obviously charmed—and why shouldn't she be? Meg thought. She'd been married for nearly fifty years to a great guy. They'd had four kids, thirteen grandchildren and twenty great-grandchildren. She had nothing to lose by appreciating Danny's wit and warmth.

Whereas Meg had ridden that slippery slope too often. No, when and *if* she got serious again, it would be with someone so entrenched in their town, their lives and his faith that she'd never have a niggle of doubt or discontent.

That's called Utopia, honey. It doesn't exist.

One glimpse of the gentle look Danny threw her way said it might if she was willing to compromise, leave her roots, spread her wings.

The thought of possibly dissolving her hard work pinched, but the thought that Danny's sons might someday inherit that sweet, crooked smile drew her.

But she'd dreamed and planned before, and despite what she *thought* she felt inside, she'd learned the hard way she couldn't exactly trust her senses. More than anything she needed to trust fully before she could give her heart. From this point forward, she intended to set the tone and the timing, a competent woman in control.

"You'll need a color for backing."

Maude's observation pulled Meg's attention back around. Danny watched her, curiosity sparking his gaze.

She moved back to his side, eyed the three options Maude had extracted from the wall of color and pointed to a tea-stained blue floral still on the shelf. "I prefer the antique look of the tea-stained background, but the clean blue and white is nice. It's fresh. More modern."

Danny studied her a moment, his face unreadable. A tiny muscle in his cheek jumped before he turned back to Maude, refusing to do battle. "The blue and white it is, then, with maybe this for the backing?" He flicked a finger to a bolt of colonial blue calico with a hint of yellow brightening the floral design; the slightly deeper tone made a good balance.

"Perfect," Maude declared.

Danny helped carry the pile of fabric to the cutting table, the soft thunks of the flipping bolts a reminder of days of old, just like that tea-stained fabric. Meg moved to the front window, the rustic wood framing an idyllic scene, a summer Sunday morning in Jamison.

Danny had chosen the white for good reason. A traveling businessman, he had no small-town ties to their time-tried community, no ingrained love for cobbled streets and worn-board walkways.

She did. Her home, her family, her life was in Allegany County. She'd gone to college locally on purpose, feeling no need to wander far from her roots.

There was nothing wrong with loving home, loving the past, clinging to family. Right?

Whither thou goest, I will go. And whither thou lodgest, I will lodge… The gentle words from the book of Ruth prickled. Ruth had been brave enough to turn her back on the safety of her homeland, her people, and accompany Naomi in her travels, a brave woman, willing to go the distance. Meg straightened her shoulders, determined to listen and discern God's will, although her stubborn Russo side was rarely comfortable with patience.

"Ready?"

Meg hauled in a breath, turned from the window-framed portrait of small-town America and nodded. "Yes. You're set?"

He hoisted a bag. "Kind of amazing to think there's enough material in here for a quilt, isn't it?"

Megan laughed. "Well, it's minus the batting."

"Say what?"

"The filler." She pointed right, where stacks of rolled batts hugged a corner.

"I need that?"

"Your grandmother will, but it's available all over. I wouldn't mail it to her. Crazy expensive."

He tipped his gaze down once more as they stepped onto Maude's creatively decorated boardwalk section. Just then Brad and Denise crossed the cobbled road a few stores down, her pregnancy obvious, a bowl-cut, towheaded preschooler racing ahead, despite Brad's warning to slow down.

Danny intercepted Meg's look and paused, a hand to her arm, as if he realized who they were—but that was impossible, wasn't it?

Not in a small town.

"Would you like to cross the street?"

Yes. Meg sighed inside, willfully hiding her angst. "Not in the least."

Danny grinned, shifted the bag and grabbed her hand. "Just for show."

His teasing look said otherwise, but if Megan was about to come face-to-face with her former fiancé, clutching Danny's hand wasn't a bad touch.

Brad's look of surprise was a little overdone, as if he hadn't seen them coming.

Please.

Denise's slightly smug expression of victory faded as Danny brought Megan's hand up for a quick kiss, one of the sweetest, most genteel public displays of affection known to mankind.

Meg willed herself not to melt on contact. "Brad, good morning. Off to church?" They weren't, she knew that from the way they were so casually dressed.

"Grabbing breakfast in town." Brad drew Denise a little closer. "Mom's kitchen is torn up, so it's a little tricky to keep Brad Junior out from underfoot."

"Understandable." Megan smiled down at the little boy, his fair face and hair more Denise than Brad.

"He's gorgeous." She said the words honestly, the little boy's beginnings rightly a thing of the past. But because she wasn't completely sweet or born yesterday, she tugged Danny forward with a teasing glance upward, meeting his gaze, inspiring his smile. She hadn't spent four consecutive years in the high school drama club for nothing. "Danny, this is Brad and his wife, Denise. I told you about them."

Danny slid into the role seamlessly, a fact she'd worry about later. "You did." He sent her a grin that said *What on Earth was he thinking?* in big, block letters before he closed the distance between them. He raised his encumbered arm in apology, his right hand gripping Meg's left. "Sorry. Don't have a free hand. You're in town for the summer?"

"Yes." Denise answered, her voice edging tart.

Meg tried unsuccessfully to squelch how good that felt.

Danny nodded, at ease and comfortable, as if he'd come out on the winning end of a long, drawn-out struggle. Which he hadn't, but his attitude and stance suggested otherwise. He shifted his gaze to the little boy who'd had enough of adult conversation and was darting down the wooden walk, bumping unsuspecting people as he barreled through. "Well, you're obviously busy…"

Brad growled and dashed after the boy, the Sunday morning stragglers impeding his way.

"And you—" Danny smiled down at Meg and squeezed her hand "—have a store to open."

"I do." Meg pulled herself from Danny's warm look with effort, even though she knew the locked gaze was manufactured for effect. She turned back to Denise, feeling suddenly sincere. "Denise, good luck with the new house. And the new baby."

"Thanks."

Walking away, Megan huffed out a deep, long, maybe-held-forever breath.

"What was that for?"

"Because I just this moment realized how glad I am not to be her."

Danny turned, his gaze resting on the disgruntled young father who obviously had little control over his preschool son. "Really?"

"I was younger."

"Hmm."

"More naive."

"Impossible."

"Hey!"

He laughed. "You know, I get that you're business savvy, I've seen that from the beginning. But I'm only starting to realize the power behind the happily-ever-after thing that controls women's decision-making process."

"What's that supposed to mean?" She stopped, turned and faced him toe to toe, pulling her hand free.

He lifted his eyes to where Brad and Denise now squabbled outside Maude's inviting entrance, then looked back at her. "You honestly considered settling for *that?*"

"You don't know anything about it." She pivoted, shoved her hands in her pockets and picked up the pace toward home.

He hurried after her. "Then tell me."

"No."

"Because?"

"It's none of your business. Look." She turned back, wishing he didn't have the power to hit so many buttons. "Everybody makes mistakes. We all have a past. The worst thing I've done is be unlucky in love." When he looked like he might comment, she raised a hand in silent request to allow her to continue.

"A lot of factors enter into romance, to love. Yes, I was younger, but not young. Yes, I wanted the dream, probably too badly because my friends had been getting married one by one. I've been a brides-maid three times, and each time I wondered if that old saying about never being a bride was true, but you know what, Danny?"

He shook his head, his gaze quiet.

"I'm done with all that. I won't pretend I'm at peace with what happened, not yet anyway, but I'm totally done letting biological clocks and great smiles sway my common sense. I've been fooled, yes, but I refuse to be fooled again. Ever." She punctuated the last word with a silent "even by you" look that he read loud and clear, his eyes saying he got the message. "So now I work, I plan, I choose. I'm the captain of my ship and no one—" she took a step forward and saw the glint in his eye, but decided she was strong enough to handle whatever he might send her way "—*no one* will steer me off course without my permission. Got it?"

"Completely." He held her gaze, a slight shadow darkening the steadfast look he maintained before he smiled. "I actually respect your stance."

"Right."

She headed home once more and felt him fall into step beside her, comfortably close, but not close enough. Her hand missed the warmth of his grip, those tight fingers, the arm-to-arm contact.

Time to change the subject. She adjusted her pace, drew a breath and decided to try to act somewhat sane, at least for the remainder of the walk home. "So, Danny Graham. What is it you do, exactly?"

Chapter Eleven

Tell her.

No way.

He couldn't, could he? Just blurt it out, here and now, walking along the street after she just threw down a challenge, drew a line in the sand?

Yes. Now. What are you waiting for?

Well, that was the question of the hour, wasn't it? He'd known all along that if he was successful, his mission would mess with her life, her goals, and here he was, ready and willing to take her down.

He'd half tell her.

He turned her way and tried not to stumble over the half truths he was about to spew. "It's kind of hard for me to say this, but you really need to know. I'm down here to scout out a retail site for my grandmother. For a candy store."

She stopped dead, face flat before confusion crinkled her eyes. "And you saw no reason to tell me that?"

"Megan, I—"

"Before I rented you the apartment next door? Before I let you walk with me, talk with me..."

Watching anger and distrust shadow her features, he decided it wasn't the best time to remind her they'd done more than walk and talk.

And it still wasn't enough. Not nearly.

She strode ahead, one hand behind her back as if literally shoving him off. Then she stopped, turned and came back, indignation replacing hurt and confusion. "You rat."

"Megs—"

"Don't 'Megs' me, Danny Graham, not now, not ever. You're just like all the rest, only you're a little better off and more practiced, which only makes me like you less." She turned away, a flip of those delightful golden brown curls her last word.

"That's not true."

She whirled back. "It's so beyond true that it could easily become your Facebook status, and everyone..." she took a step closer "...who logs onto your page..." closer yet, a finger raised to jab him in the chest, not once but twice "...will understand what a bozo you are with one quick glance." She looked very angry and way too cute for her own good.

"Megs, I didn't lie to you. I just didn't tell you why I was here, exactly."

She waved a hand as she turned the corner to her store and their apartments, her footsteps on the wooden stairs sharp and staccato. "Lies of omission are still lies."

"Meg…"

Slam.

The sharp crack of the candy store door left no doubt that Meg was done with him, at least for the moment. Possibly for the day. The week?

He refused to think in terms of forever because he never thought in terms of forever, at least not until he'd arrived in Jamison.

He stood stock-still for long beats of the clock, staring at the door, wavering on what to do.

He'd told her. At least in part. That was good, right?

You wimped out. Should have told her everything.

He would, he decided. Once she calmed down about this whole candy store thing, he'd confess who he was. Who his grandmother was. Surely that would help Meg understand his conundrum.

He headed to his door to gather his keys and get away from there, away from her, away from the stark look of condemnation he read in her eyes, knowing he, too, had deceived her. After he promised he wouldn't.

Would she hate him?

She couldn't.

Could she?

Rounding the corner of the house, a bevy of activity drew his attention to the Victorian-styled bird condo, peeps and chirps of tiny finches marking their devotion and industry, the work-together

attitude that kept them forging on, moving ahead
and singing all the while they built their nests.

He saw his family business that way, hard won
and hard fought. Years of struggle mixed with years
of prosperity to mark Grandma Mary's history. But
they'd hung on, hung together, working through war
years and bad economies.

"Ability is what gets you to the top. Character is
what keeps you there." Abraham Lincoln's inspira-
tional words were one of Grandma's oft-used quotes,
and Danny thought he'd done a decent job of achiev-
ing the drive and character his family worked to
inspire. Seeing Meg's reaction, realizing he should
have come clean from the beginning, made him see
that the character aspects of the quote might still
need work.

The old man's weathered gaze from church came
back to him, the look he'd bestowed on Danny as
he'd accepted the hymnbook.

He'd known, somehow.

Not who Danny was legally, but who he was spir-
itually. The wizened look had offered acceptance,
knowledge and advice, with never a word spoken.

Danny ducked inside, grabbed his keys, climbed
into the nondescript rental and backed out of the
drive, distancing himself from Meg's distrust.

A heron rose up from a small creek bordering
Route 19, the majesty of pterosaur-type wings a link
with days gone by, things of old.

Heading south, he realized that maybe the clean

blue and white hadn't been the best choice in fabric, and he'd never gotten Meg the promised walnut-maple twist roll.

He was a jerk, plain and simple.

Danny walked into an east-facing card and gift shop on Main Street in Wellsville about two hours later and came face-to-face with the same faded blue eyes he'd met in church that morning. "We meet again."

The older man smiled, happy to see him, maybe happy to see anyone, the store way too quiet for a Sunday afternoon while people milled on the sidewalk, June's gentle weather beckoning. "Ayuh. I was just tellin' the missus that maybe we shouldn't open on Sundays anymore, that there wasn't enough business to make sense, but she's a stubborn old coot."

"Am not." The older woman stepped in from a small room beyond, her look saying she'd heard all this before. "And don't you go filling this young man's mind with all kinds of things. He's new around here."

"And you know that because?" Danny shifted his attention to her.

"Maude McGinnity is one of my best friends."

"Ah."

"And she weren't gossipin', neither, our Maude doesn't do that, never did, but she was explaining to me how you came to be walkin' with Megan Russo this morning."

Danny flinched, not wanting to consider the option of never walking with Megan again. She'd forgive him in time. Right?

Right up until you tell her the rest, about how you represent one of the biggest candy conglomerates this side of the Mississippi.

The woman swept him a glance, sighed deeply, then leaned against the wall.

Danny surged forward. "Are you okay?"

"Kate, you havin' one of them spells?" The old man struggled to rise, his joints uncooperative. Danny was uncertain whom to help first, but he figured if the elderly gentleman rose, they could both help the woman.

She straightened, the look of discomfort erased by a smile. "Nothing to get all steamed up about, boys. Sit down, old man, before you fall down." She took the sting out of the words with a gentle pat to his shoulder, the look and touch meant to reassure.

Danny nearly sighed relief out loud, happy to avoid the drama of an ambulance call as he realized that neither of these two was in great health.

The old woman motioned him left. "Are you looking for a gift for someone?"

He should have been if he wanted to regain Meg's favor at any point in time. "Yes."

"Your wife?"

"Not married."

"Ah." He and the old man both noted the heightened note in her voice, the sharp look of interest she shot Danny's way.

"Don't be matchmakin' on this young man, Kate McGee. He's not here forever and we don't need no more of our young folks traipsin' off to parts unknown."

"Oh, piffle, Jed, you're just steamed because our Kathleen is the only one of ours that stayed hereabouts, but young folks need to go where the jobs are, where there's opportunity. You know that."

"Bah."

She rolled her eyes and turned back to Danny. "Now, about that gift."

"Something pretty for a girl who loves old-fashioned things."

Kate's look of satisfaction said his description came as no surprise, giving Danny another glimpse of small-town living and the light-year speed of information travel.

He walked to the far side of the store, noting that the darker wall color shadowed the sale space, making the store appear less inviting.

Kate McGee walked alongside him, her measured step obviously painful. "Dang hip is not to be trusted these days," she grumbled, as she reached to the third shelf along the south wall. "This punched tinware is nice, and we've got it in all sorts of colors. That dark red is a favorite."

Danny reached beyond the tinware to a ceramic bowl decked with hand-painted flowers, the colors reminding him of that material Meg had pointed out that morning. What had she called it? Tea-stained.

The bowl bore that same soft beige background, the smattering of blue flowers and green leaves reflective of the calico, but the bowl had tiny sprigs of white flowers as well, the white offering a hint of light to the more muted colors around it.

The effect was beautiful. Soft. Winsome. Meg.

"I'll take this."

She nodded approval at his choice, then reached up, a hint of discomfort marring her features from even that simple movement. "There's more up there to match."

Danny hesitated, then shrugged. "Just the bowl for now."

"He ain't in *that* much trouble, Kate." The old man chortled from behind the counter, his words spiking memories of Meg's look, her gaze, the distrust he'd placed there.

Reconsidering, Danny turned back to the display. "Maybe I should check out another piece or two."

Kate grinned.

A creamer, sugar bowl and candy dish later, Danny watched as the elderly man worked uncooperative fingers to wrap each piece in tissue before placing them in thin, white gift boxes.

He leaned forward, unsure, but knowing he had to ask. "You folks ever think about selling this store?"

The woman looked surprised.

The man didn't. "Yup. More lately with how hard it is for us to get around, but there ain't a lot of people buying stores hereabouts. Least with the new business Walker Electronics is bringin' in, things should start gettin' better, but yeah." He paused. "We've talked about it plenty."

"I'm interested in buying it." Danny watched their reaction go from interest to caution. "I've been looking for retail space here on Main Street, but I wanted something that faced east and there's nothing vacant on this side."

"So you came lookin' for someone a little down on their luck?" The old man drew himself up, suspicion clouding his features.

"I did." Danny faced him, determined to be totally up front. "But only because it seemed like it might work well for both of us. My family is prepared to pay cash for the site. We'd like to be in by September, and I know that's kind of a rush—"

"Can't be soon enough for me if the price is right," the old man declared. He moved forward and held out his hand. "I'm Jed McGee and this here's my wife, Kate, but you know that already."

Danny nodded and shook both their hands.

"What kind of price are we talking, young man?"

Danny named a price that made their eyes widen, and he could almost hear the lecture his father would give him later, knowing you never offered top dollar straight off.

But Jed and Kate McGee didn't have a lot of time left for games, and Danny didn't feel like toying with their future. While both appeared to have their ailments, their sweet natures belied any suffering they might be feeling, a great lesson in and of itself.

"Mother, you'd have time to get that hip fixed up if we didn't have to run the store every day."

Kate nodded. "And that cataract surgery you been putting off."

Danny's heart melted a little more. They'd put off surgeries that might help them because they couldn't afford time away from the business. "If you're interested, I can have my attorney draw up a contract. He can fax it to me and I can present it to you tomorrow."

"You need thinking time, Kate?"

She eyed Danny, made a decision and shook her head. "Nope."

"Me, either. We'd a done this years ago if anyone offered."

Danny smiled and shook Jed's hand. "Then I'm glad no one did."

"What are you planning to put in here?" Kate asked, her gaze curious.

Danny almost sighed. "A candy store."

"But ain't you livin' alongside—"

"Yes."

"Oh." Distress darkened Kate's features. "Does Megan know?"

Oh, she knew all right. Danny frowned and shrugged. "Yes." He shifted his gaze toward the packaged gifts, letting his gesture explain further. "She knows."

"She's worked hard up there," the old man reminded them both. As if Danny needed reminding.

He nodded. "She has and she's got a great business. I'm hoping that my place won't have much effect on her store."

"Come winter, the littlest drop in sales affects everyone," John told him.

Danny knew that. He'd checked the local figures, and if you were off the beaten path, the downturn shift in winter income became downright scary. Meg had explained the ice cream and festival business for that very reason, to help offset the slow months of January through March.

But seeing Jed and Kate, he understood that his grandma faced a similar challenge as she aged, and she was determined to give back to the community that fostered her mother's business and independence. He had no choice but to go on, regardless of the fallout. Knowing that made him feel like less of a heel, but only slightly. "I'm hoping we'll both thrive. And Jamison is such a tourist draw, Meg will continue to have interstate trade that we don't get down here."

"Precious few people travel I-86 in the winter, and that's only if they have to, and few of them stop for anything other than gas," John informed him.

"Although I won't say we're not delighted to have that road nice and close like it is. Weren't easy for folks to get into this region for a long time."

John's assertion rang true. Part of the reason the Allegheny foothills area had pitched downhill economically was the poor accessibility. Eventually the new interstate and major roads were rebuilt, inviting greater access to the area. Opportunities were increasing.

Perfect for a business slated for Main Street, Wellsville.

He swallowed hard and reached for his bags. "I'll have my lawyer draw up the papers." He made the statement a question, head angled slightly.

"Yes," Kate said.

"Yes." Jed nodded, his consent firmer than Kate's.

"The only thing I ask is that we keep this confidential for a few weeks." Danny turned his look to the street. "The store is for my grandmother, and I want to make sure I've got everything set before we make things public."

"Mother and I know how to keep things quiet."

Kate stepped forward. "There's no funny business goin' on, is there?"

Danny shook his head. "I assure you, there's not. And feel free to have a lawyer go over the contract I bring over. It's always wise to seek legal counsel when you're talking this kind of money. We've got nothing to hide and because it's cash, it should be a simple transfer of title. There are no liens against the property?"

"None." Jed straightened his shoulders, proud. "Mother and I've been together nearly fifty-four years and we've paid our bills, every one of them."

That declaration didn't surprise Danny in the least. He reached out a hand to shake theirs. "I'll be by later tomorrow."

"We'll be here."

Danny headed back to his car, the weight of the bags a reminder of Meg's anger and mistrust.

But beyond her hurt feelings lay the simple fact that she was entrenched in her small-town existence and he had a job to do. They were at opposite ends of the spectrum, their jobs allowing little geographic compromise. He'd known that going in, and still he'd let himself become involved.

The memory of their sweet kiss spawned a chain of what-ifs, but he had to be sensible. His job required travel, and he'd seen Meg with her family. They were close-knit, and Ben's needs were a focal point for all of them.

She couldn't leave.

He couldn't stay.

Exactly the reason why he should walk away now. Leave it alone. Meg deserved someone who would put her needs first, love her and cherish her all of her days. She'd already been burned twice by men too stupid to realize the treasure they held.

And yet he couldn't deny the wash of peace he'd

felt that morning, the century-old hymns and flick-
ering candles a quiet summons, the calm of the sur-
roundings easing his city-wearied soul.

Jed McGee's faded gaze came to mind. The old
man had put off surgery to help his wife, and she'd
put off surgery to help him. Their "Gift of the Magi"
existence offered heartfelt inspiration, a living,
breathing example from the book of Corinthians.

Being with Meg inspired those feelings in him, a
whisper of possibilities that refused to be silenced.

Strains of the Four Seasons' "Candy Girl" interrupted his thoughts. Danny grabbed the phone.
"Mary Clare, what's up?"

Long seconds of silence said too much. Danny
gripped the phone tighter. "Sis, what's going on?
Are you okay?"

Another stretch of near silence said she was fighting tears.

The Mary Clare he grew up with never cried, and
if she did succumb to tears, they were generally tears
of anger. With Christian's death they flowed more
often, a fact that unnerved him, mostly because there
was nothing he could do to offer solace.

"We've got trouble."

Bad reception garbled her voice, breaking up her
words. "In Philly? Which store? Market Street or
University City?"

"Uni—" Crackle. Snap. Crackle.

"Mare, you there? Hello?"

"I've—" Dead air space followed, leaving Danny

clutching the phone, vexed and distraught, ready to make the five-hour drive to Philly that moment. He pulled the car off the side of the road, climbed out and held the phone aloft, looking for better reception.

No magical bars appeared.

What had he promised her? That he'd come at a moment's notice if she needed him? If he left now he could be there before dark with the extended daylight, and help her with whatever she needed.

By the time he pulled the car into his parking spot at Megan's, he'd imagined a myriad images about what might have gone wrong in Philly, with its recent upsurge in crime.

As he climbed out of the car, his phone rang again; it was his mother's ringtone. "Mom? Have you heard from Mary Clare? Is she okay? What's going on?"

"She's fine, Daniel. They had a police intervention just outside the campus store and had to cordon it off for a while, but everything's clear now."

"What kind of intervention?"

His mother didn't mince words, but then, she never did. "A drug deal gone bad."

His protective instincts soared. "You're kidding."

"I'm not, but everything's all right."

"And Mary Clare's okay? Physically? Emotionally?"

"Yes." Merrilee's calm was a gift passed down

from Grandma, two industrious ladies that refused to allow life to daunt them.

Like Meg, he realized.

"She's a little shaken from the adrenaline rush, but the Philadelphia Police Department stepped in and took care of everything."

"Mom, I—"

Merilee interrupted him before he got any further. "I'm going to tell you the same thing I told your father. If either one of you were handling this, I wouldn't be hopping on a plane or driving down to hold your hand. I'd expect you to follow police procedures, increase security—"

"And Mary Clare has already done that," Danny admitted.

"Exactly. No one likes this kind of thing, but between the campus police and the P.P.D., the store is being well covered. And if we go charging in as though your sister can't handle this, it's a show of no confidence. She can't afford that."

"But—"

"No buts." The tap, tap, tap of a pencil said his mother's mind was working furiously. "She's not in danger, she's just flustered. Let her sprout those wings, Danny. They got clipped last year when Christian died, but we need to do whatever it takes to bolster her. Not baby her."

Danny bit back a sigh. His mother's wisdom was easier in word than deed, but she was right. He knew that. Still…

"Have you found a site for the tribute store, yet?"

He accepted the businesslike change of subject with grace. "I did. It's a perfect location, facing east in Wellsville on Main Street. You'll love it."

"Excellent."

"So. You'll keep me posted on the Philly situation?"

"Of course. And you keep us informed on the Wellsville deal. Have we cut a contract yet?"

"Tomorrow."

A hint of relief colored her tone. "Good. Grandma's champing at the bit to come down there but I keep putting her off with work here, which hasn't been hard to do with you and your sister gone."

"I've got the preliminary plans all set once I find a contractor, but that shouldn't be hard."

"And if you've got a few days to come home, that's fine, Daniel. Once the site is purchased and the contractor in place, you really don't need to be there every day, do you?"

The fact that he wanted to be here every day wasn't something he would share with his mother just yet. "Not necessarily, but we'll see. I need to make sure everything goes smoothly. And you'll keep me updated about Mary Clare's status?"

"I will. Right now our job is to trust God, Mary Clare and the P.P.D."

"I'm trying."

She gave a short laugh, part lament. "Try harder. You and your father are wonderful men but too protective for your own good. It's time to join us ladies in the new millennium, okay?"

"I get it, Mom."

"Good. Love you."

"You, too." He hung up the phone, weighing her words. He knew his sister needed to step out on her own, but drug deals? Police? Elevated security?

Let go and let God.

That's what Grandma would say. She'd told him to trust God, a concept he'd neglected these past years, but after being surrounded by the peace and quiet of Jamison and Wellsville, and the outpouring of congenial people, he realized he was out of practice through his own fault, a situation he intended to change starting now.

Meg's lights were out, the candy store and ice cream window closed for the day.

He'd see her tomorrow. Apologize. Explain. She'd either forgive him for who he was or she wouldn't, but he couldn't let it slide any longer. With the store site chosen, word might get out. He wanted her to hear it from him. It was the least he could do.

Chapter Twelve

Danny Graham was really Daniel Graham Romesser, vice president in charge of Eastern Region marketing for Grandma Mary's Candies, one of the biggest and best candy conglomerates in the country.

Meg was still trying to digest that information the next morning, half wishing she hadn't looked him up on Google. But she had, and the idea that Grandma Mary's intended to build a store in Allegany County bit deep. She already worked night and day all summer and fall to offset the weaker months of winter. What would she have to do to survive with a competitor minutes away?

Fear clenched her heart. She'd worked hard to gain ground, to become a money-making enterprise. With one swipe of a pen, Danny Graham might wipe that all out. Small businesses operated on a thin profit margin, a concept pretty boys like him might not understand.

But Meg got it because she lived it. By the time

she met Hannah to plan the week's fudge and cookie schedule in preparation for the onslaught of July festivals, she was ready to burst.

"You're sure?" Hannah hiked a sympathetic brow in Megan's direction as she set out fudge pans, checking off the list in her hands as she went. "You didn't make a mistake? Pull up the wrong Danny Graham? It's not an uncommon name."

"Yes, it's the right guy. I double-checked by going to Images, and there he was." She didn't add that the shots of Danny in his corporate suit and tie were to-die-for or that the one with a very pretty girl in a great designer dress made her rue her full-length calicos.

Nope. Obviously Danny's other life encompassed a laundry list of things she wouldn't, shouldn't and couldn't afford to care about.

"You need to talk to him. Straighten this out. And he did tell you why he was in town."

Meg hauled the big mixer bowl to the corner and began tossing in ingredients for molasses cookies, an old-fashioned town favorite at festival time. "Right. Yesterday. After spying on my store for weeks."

"Spying?"

Meg shrugged, counting scoops of flour. "He might have been spying. We don't know."

"If he was, I think he was checking out the girl, not the store." Hannah offered her wise counsel while she inventoried ingredients stock for fudge production. "This is Grandma Mary's we're talking. They're huge."

"Tell me something I don't know," Meg grumped back. "And I can't believe he didn't tell me right off, let me know what he was here for. Of all the underhanded, low-down—"

"Mm-hmm." Hannah kept her face pseudoserious as she stacked cooling racks on a bakery cart. "I'm minding my own business, but it's pretty funny to see two eligible, intelligent adults tiptoe around each other like adversaries in a boxing ring when their only crime is running similar businesses."

"It's not funny, it's exasperating. Frustrating. Annoying."

"I get it. You sure you guys can't entertain the option of a merger? Because it makes perfect sense to me."

The thought of merging with Danny Graham had a special ring to it, providing all the more reason to shut the thought down. Hadn't she gone into summer determined to put business first, and then there she was, willingly spinning on a romantic merry-go-round only to realize the ride was more like the bumper cars. Meg hated bumper cars.

"And kiss my independence goodbye?" She shook her head and set out cookie sheets with more vehemence than was absolutely necessary. "No way do I want to manage a store for someone else after I've worked so hard to build my own business. I can't imagine having to answer to corporate execs—"

"Like Danny."

"Especially Danny." Meg let aggravation tinge her tone purposely. "Being bossed around by a 'silver spoon' who got handed his job and title from Mom and Dad isn't my idea of success."

"Silver spoon?"

Oh, no.

Meg turned around and wished the floor could swallow her.

"You know who I am?"

"Daniel Graham Romesser, heir apparent to Grandma Mary's Candies? Yes. I checked you out on the internet last night. You could have told me that yesterday."

"You didn't give me a chance, remember? You stomped off and slammed the door in my face."

She huffed and turned back toward her work production area. "Hardly in your face when you were on the sidewalk."

"Close enough." He moved forward until Meg had to turn his way. Meet his gaze.

"I'm not a silver spoon, Meg, and for your information…" He stepped closer, looking none too pleased and more than a little insulted. "…I've worked my way up the chain of command at Grandma Mary's after completing a business degree at Wharton, so the thought that I've been handed anything by anyone is ludicrous."

"Wharton's a great school," Hannah acknowledged. "I went to Penn, so we might have been neighbors."

Meg appreciated Hannah's attempt to normalize the situation, but she'd dug her own hole. Now to figure a way out of it—

"I didn't mean to insult you."

"But you did."

"Danny, get serious."

He folded his arms, the standoff obvious. "I'm quite serious."

"You were born into a family with an existing business that already had multi-million-dollar sales. It grew exponentially while you were a kid. Can you deny that you walked into a pretty solid situation? Really?"

He stared at her, then swept her store a studied look. "You know, I've admired what you've done here from the first moment I set foot in the place. Your eye for balance, for placement, the quality and quantities, the balance of ice cream versus chocolate and cookies. It's all wonderful and indicative of a keen business sense, but—" he moved closer "—it might be nice—" closer yet "—to have a little respect come my way in return. Just because you built yourself from the ground up doesn't negate what I've done for my family business. And you know what, Meg?"

Looking up into eyes that had gone from sunset gray to Pittsburgh steel, she shook her head.

"I get that you've been burned. I get that you've got issues with guys, but none of that gives you the right to insult me or my family business. That's just plain low."

"I'm sorry."

He shook his head, stepped back, hands up, palms out. "Right. Well, here's what we'll do, Meg. Let's just forget this conversation ever happened, okay? I'll let myself out, I'll spend the remainder of my weeks here as little as possible and pretty soon this will just be another summer laid to rest."

His words stammered her heart, her gut. Or was it the look that said she'd gone irrevocably over the top this time?

She watched him leave and tried to calm the adrenaline rush and the ensuing speeded-up pulse, but with Hannah darting sympathetic looks her way, it proved impossible.

Hannah jerked her thumb toward the door. "I've got to head to the library. I'll be back at five. You're good?"

"Crystal will be here to run the counter any minute. We're fine, thanks."

Hannah's look asked more than her words, but Meg couldn't address either right now, not and maintain her composure after what just happened.

She'd insulted Danny and his family with her quick words. She'd maligned his integrity in a bout of self-absorbed anger, and Danny Graham had just quietly walked out of her life. Since the experience wasn't exactly new, why on Earth did it hurt this much? She barely knew the guy, right?

Quiet surrounded her once Hannah left, leaving her too much time to mull, even with the big mixer blending molasses cookie dough. Speaking of which…

Meg turned, shut off the mixer, pressed the clutch and changed the speed before setting the timer at five minutes. Two more batches and she'd be done mixing for the day, then the rote work of filling cookie trays by hand would keep her hopping as she produced hundreds of cookies in her smallish ovens.

Grasping the garbage bag, she tied the top, hoisted it and headed to the small Dumpster out back, her attention torn between the heavy bag listing her right and wanting to know if Danny's car was gone, hoping to avoid another confrontation.

She missed the bottom step completely, stepping off into air, the heavy bag wrenching her right while her left arm groped for the handrail with no success.

The crack of forearm bone followed by a fiery shot of pain to her shoulder and neck made her cry out, but since no one was around to hear, it really didn't make all that much difference.

\> Danny glared at the seat beside him, realizing he'd left his cell phone at the apartment. He made a K-turn on a quiet side road and retraced his path north, trying to make sense of his anger and Meg's disparagement and coming up short.

Sure she had a right to be irritated and concerned, but ridiculing him and the family business struck low. Could he help his birthright? His family?

Ridiculous.

Working your way up when your last name matches the company's owners might not be as tough as you make out, dude.

The internal reminder struck a chord. That *had* played a part in his success. For decades he'd been groomed to become an executive, then owner of the family business. His parents' work ethic became his, but he had the incentive of a large corporation falling into his lap at some point in time.

Meg was right about the circumstance, but wrong about her analogy. He hadn't been, nor ever would be, a silver spoon.

He pulled into the stone drive on his side of the house, jumped out of the car, glad that Hannah had left, embarrassed that she'd witnessed the heated exchange he had with Meg. He was more than ready to grab his phone and be on his way when a small sound drew his attention to the backyard. He headed around the corner and spotted Meg on the ground, the garbage bag off to the side, the sheen of tears and pain unmistakable.

Fear grabbed his heart.

"Hey, hey, hey, Megs." He half crooned the words at a dead run. He dropped to her side and slipped an arm around her shoulders to hold her, cradle her. "What happened? Are you okay? Are you hurt?"

The wince when he touched her right arm provided all the evidence he needed. "Oh, Meg."

She buried her face into his shirt, and he tried to pretend it didn't feel absolutely wonderful to have her there, despite the reason why, that it didn't feel like the most natural thing in the world to hold her, cherish her, comfort her.

He allowed himself a few moments, but knew they didn't have time to revel in these feelings. Meg needed medical help. "Come on, honey, let's get you up." He stood and braced his hands around her waist, lifting her to her feet.

Crystal Murphy appeared at the back door. "Hey, Meg." One glance had her opening the door with a bang. "Meg, are you all right? Are you okay?"

Danny kept an arm snugged around Meg's waist and shook his head. "She's hurt. I'm going to run her down to Jones Memorial, see what's up. But from the look of it—" he nodded where Meg's right arm took a decidedly awkward turn "—I'm guessing we've got a broken arm."

"We?"

Danny met the pained but still slightly stubborn look Meg shot him and nodded. "Friends share their successes and their problems."

Friends?

Meg heard the word and thought back to the

moment before time and space disappeared from under her feet, her attention split because she'd hurt Danny, and the last thing she wanted to do was hurt Danny.

She looked up at Crystal. "Can you cover the dough that just finished in the big mixer?"

Crystal nodded. "Of course."

"It'll be fine until I get back, and then I'll mix up the other varieties." She hesitated, frowned, then shrugged. "Right now I'm wishing I'd trained you on baking cookies."

Crystal grimaced. "I could try, but…"

"We'll worry about this when we get back," Danny told them both. "Let's get to the hospital, find out how bad it is and then we'll attack the work schedule. Hannah's working tonight, right?"

"Yes."

"And your parents are both at work."

She nodded, biting her lip to stave off tears, the pain in her arm shooting upward. "Yes."

"Well, then it's lucky you've got Crystal and me."

Right then Meg wasn't feeling all that lucky. Her right arm throbbed in protest as she lowered herself into his car.

But she couldn't deny how good it felt to have Danny run to her rescue, take charge, hold her and help her. Jane Austen couldn't have scripted this better, so she'd have to work double time to remember why falling for Danny was a bad idea.

Right now he was a dream come true, his gaze

focused on the road before them when he wasn't casting concerned glances her way with every bump and wiggle. "You're doing okay?"

"Fine."

She wasn't close to fine, the pain a fiery torment even with her left hand cushioning her right arm from movement. Glancing down, she prayed it wasn't broken, maybe twisted or sprained, a setback of a couple of days, a week maximum.

The remembered snap of bone said she was wrong.

She prayed she was right, because if her arm was broken, she'd have to pay someone else to help with production. That option would just about erase her winter cushion of funds.

Morning traffic and a construction project on Route 19 slowed their progress. Danny glared at a red light in a small town, his fingers tapping the steering column, annoyed. Meg swept the drumming fingers a pointed glance. "Are you this impatient when you drive in New York? Or Philly?"

He sent her a little smile as if appreciating the change of subject. "No. Yes. Maybe. I'm not usually taking a beautiful girl to the emergency room, so comparisons are unfair."

"Thank you."

He arched a brow, inquisitive, his gaze on the road, the traffic commanding his attention.

"For saying I'm beautiful."

He smiled. "Nothing the mirror doesn't tell you every day."

"Mirrors are tricky things."

"Not in your case, Megs."

The sincerity in his voice bathed her. His calm, take-charge attitude allowed her to see a different side to him. This Danny wasn't schmoozing, placating or working a deal to his advantage. He was doing what a good executive did: assessing and dealing with whatever came his way.

He pulled into the emergency lot, parked the car and hurried around back to help her out. "Easy now. You want a wheelchair?"

"For my arm?"

Worry darkened his features before he nodded and shrugged. "Sorry."

"I'm not." A little shy, she tipped her gaze up to his, relieved that treatment was steps away, her words triggered by his obvious concern. "I'm glad you found me."

He met her gaze and couldn't help himself. He leaned down, feathered her lips a kiss and slipped his arm around her waist while she balanced her bad arm with her good one. "Me, too. Although I was pretty mad at you an hour ago."

She flushed, embarrassed.

His hand around her waist offering a comforting squeeze. "Let's go get that arm fixed, okay?"

"You don't think it's really broken, do you?"

"Yup."

"And your medical degree is from?"

"Experience. I broke mine in freshman soccer. Six weeks in a cast, missed most of the season. It was not a good year."

"Six weeks?"

He led her toward the pleasant-looking woman in the triage area. "Yes."

"You've got to be wrong. There's no way I can have my right arm in a cast during the six busiest weeks of my summer. It's impossible."

He leaned a little closer. "Wasn't it you who told me that with God, all things are possible?"

She sputtered. "I didn't for the life of me think you were listening."

"And yet, I was."

The nurse halted their conversation by going through preliminaries with Meg, a step that seemed way too long for Danny's peace of mind, but when they got to the insurance information, he scowled at the card she handed over. "That's your plan?"

"High deductibles increase affordability," she told him. "Insurance is crazy expensive when you're in business on your own. I went five years without it until I felt financially sound enough to buy this."

It wasn't great coverage. Danny recognized the company as one who provided significant help only in catastrophic cases. Simple things like E.R. visits, well visits, painful broken bones?

Meg would pay most of the cost out of pocket, and that angered him. He really had little idea what a small business owner went through because he'd been able to skip that part of the journey, his path prepaved.

She'd been wrong about his elevated status but correct in her assumption that he'd never had to travel her road except in theory, which meant little in the book of life.

"It's a clean break and we've reduced the bend in the radius, but it won't be a fast fix," the E.R. doctor explained nearly an hour later. "Sorry." She added the last in response to Meg's chagrined expression.

"Is there an arm version of a walking cast?"

The doctor shook her head. "Afraid not. I've correctly positioned the break and applied the temporary splint. We're going to sling it for you and I've sent a prescription to the pharmacy for pain. Here's the card for Southern Tier Orthopedics—you'll need to call them and set up an appointment for Wednesday or Thursday. They'll set the bone and apply a long-term cast."

"Long term as in…?"

"Six weeks, more or less."

Meg grimaced, an act that brought Danny to her side. "Are you in pain?"

"Mad."

"Ah." He bent and met her gaze. "It's not the end of the world, you know."

"No?" She sat up straighter and faced him while the doctor stepped out to confer with a nurse, needing Danny to see reality from her point of view. "This is my busy season, my bottom line. A small business like mine depends on regular customers and the tourist trade. If I can't produce goods to sell, I've got nothing."

"You've got friends." He maintained a steadfast look, unfazed, unflappable, bordering on annoying. "There are people here who will help. You know that."

"They've got lives of their own, Danny."

"True, but—"

"Hannah's a great help, but she's running the library so she's only available part-time. Crystal's a sweetheart but she knows nothing about the candy-making or cookie-baking side of things. She's a counter girl who also works at the Tops Market in Wellsville. I'm lucky if she can give me twenty hours a week, and that's only because she's desperate for college money and loves to work. The festival girls work full-time and man the weekend booths to make extra tuition money."

"And then there's me."

"You?"

He splayed his hands as if the answer was obvious. "I'm available for the next four weeks at least."

"Get help from the competition?"

A tiny smile, half smirk, half teasing, brightened his gaze. "This way I can glean insider information, see what makes Colonial Candy Kitchen tick. Besides the beautiful owner, of course."

The doctor returned, handed Meg instructions and then swept the arm a glance, her tone stern. "And don't think you can use it just because it's not hurting as much. Keep it immobile until you see the orthopedist. No funny stuff. Got it?"

"We'll make sure of it, Doctor." Danny reached out an arm to brace Meg as she slid off the table. She winced when her feet touched the floor. He bent again, anxious. "Are you okay?"

"Aggravated."

"In other words, normal."

"Basically." She thanked the doctor and said goodbye before pulling her attention back to Danny. "Did you mean what you said?"

"Which time?"

"Ha-ha."

"About helping you?" Danny stretched his arms out, flexed his shoulders, a move that made her remember just how good it felt to be sheltered in those arms, held against that chest a couple of hours ago, a totally stellar experience other than the pulsating pain in her broken arm.

Danny held the door open, then did the same when they got to the car. He leaned in, tugged her seat belt into place and kissed her mouth, a gesture so sweet, so beautifully natural. He tapped her nose with his finger, grinned and went back to their conversation once he'd circled the car and climbed in. "Yes. I can oversee things here. My parents have the company well in hand and expected me to be tied up getting Grandma's store set, so I'm available. For work, that is."

"Don't think for one minute I was considering anything else." Meg shot him a look of warning that melted into a smile when he reached across the seat and touched her face, her cheek, her hair.

His look spoke volumes, his deep gray eyes reflecting his concern, his affection. "Honey, if I don't have you considering something else after four weeks of working side by side, then I need a refresher course in romance. Did they have that at Alfred, Megs?"

"My track record indicates I either flunked the course or skipped it entirely."

He laughed. "Good point. So we're going to do a little role reversal. I'm the student. You're the teacher."

"I'm going to show the vice president of Grandma Mary's how to make candy? And cookies?"

"Exactly. You made a good point earlier."

She flushed from within, heat spreading up her neck to her face. "Listen, I—"

"Don't apologize again. I get that you were venting, and I probably appear to be a silver spoon. I'm not, but I realized today I'm not experienced in the day-to-day grind of a small business because our company was large before I was born. And even helping set up our franchise operations, I'm not involved in the constant push to make a store successful, to pay the bills. Consider this a favor to me, a crash course in small business with no tuition."

"You don't mind helping? Really?"

Right now, glancing right, seeing the look of hope tinged with discomfort, he not only didn't mind helping, there was nothing in the world that would stop him. She needed him, he'd be there.

A warm, sweet feeling of being in the right place at the right time, a gentle God moment, made him feel…good. Peaceful. At one with the world.

Was that silly?

He'd help her. Take time with her. She was hurt, he was available, an easy equation with no underlying goals messing it up. But the thought of working side by side with Meg for the next month made his heart pump faster in anticipation. For this four weeks, give or take, she was his.

And he liked that. A lot.

Chapter Thirteen

"I'll preheat the oven," Meg announced, as they entered her store kitchen through the back door.

"You'll sit." The look on Danny's face broached no argument. Meg rolled her eyes.

"I can manage turning a knob with my left hand." She waved her left hand in the air, demonstrating its usefulness.

"Then you can manage sitting and telling me how to set the oven. It's not rocket science, right?" He crossed the kitchen after plunking her into a chair and eyed the oven. "What temperature?"

"Three-fifty."

"Convection?"

"Yes."

"Which means what?"

"The internal fan blows to keep the heat evenly circulated for multiple trays of cookies."

He nodded, adjusted the temperature setting, then stepped back. "Isn't this oven small for your volume?"

She shrugged, wondering how anyone could feel this good with a yet-to-be-set broken arm, and pretty sure the euphoria was inspired by the really cute guy in her kitchen and not the mild pain pill. "Yes. I do the cookies as a side, kind of like an all-season ice cream stand. Cookies do steady volume all twelve months, and they freeze well, so that's an advantage. Stand-up rack ovens are crazy expensive, but I hope to install one in two to three years. Then I can approach bigger venues like the schools and hospital about supplying them daily."

"Good plan," Danny agreed. "So." He turned, eyed the mixer, and shifted up a brow. "What's first?"

Meg talked him through detaching the big mixing bowl, emptying it, washing it and replacing it on the industrial mixer chassis. "While this new batch mixes, you can fill two trays of molasses cookies and slide them into the oven once the temperature gets to three-fifty."

"I'm on it."

Crystal came around from the front just then, swooped in and gave Meg a gentle hug. "Are you okay?"

Meg grimaced. "I'm broken. I get to see the orthopedist for a cast in two days."

"Oh, Meg."

"She'll be fine." Danny grabbed a gold and brown floral calico apron, slipped it over his head and tied it in back, the move making both girls smile. "This way she gets to teach me the ins and outs of small-scale production."

"Grandma Mary's ads say they make small-batch candy, just like Grandma used to," Meg reminded him. "Are you saying they don't?"

Danny sent a look around the diminutive kitchen. "Size is relative, and I just signed on to take a crash course in candy making, Meg-style. Oven's ready. What's next?"

"The cookie sheets are hanging on the wall behind you. Each one holds nine cookies."

"I love huge cookies."

The little boy appreciation in his voice made Meg grin. "Everyone does. Use the one-third cup scoop measure that's…" She laughed when he brandished the scoop aloft, an apron-wearing, modern-day Zorro, the apron not diminishing the good-looking man behind it in the least. And the stainless-steel-measuring-cup sword?

Delightful.

"You fenced?"

He made a face. "Nope. Soccer and track during high school. I wasn't solid enough to make the Penn teams. But I worked during high school, too. I actually ran the counter at the Williamsville store."

"Williamsville?"

He dipped the measuring cup into the molasses cookie dough and lifted it. "Yes, Williamsville. That's where I'm from. Like this?"

"Exactly. You catch on fast."

He glanced around before transferring his gaze to her. "Once again, not rocket science."

"Domestic science."

He scooped the dough a touch awkwardly at first, but had the swing of it by tray two. Once he had those in the oven, he shifted a brow to Meg. "Time?"

"Fourteen minutes."

"Got it. Now what?"

"We make chocolate chip dough."

"And we sample it?"

She laughed, his hopeful look putting her in mind of sweet little boys with cookie-dough faces, mops of curls and cool little shirts covered with dinosaurs and trucks. She sent him a scolding look. "Not 'til it's done. And should I lecture you on the dangers of raw egg?"

"Not to a guy who loves Caesar salad, steak tartare and French silk frosting. I don't listen to any of that stuff anyway. They change their minds every week. So, the recipe?"

"Right here." Meg tapped her head.

"Well, for this little partnership to work, Megs, we're going to write these down so I have them available. If you're napping or resting or at a doctor's appointment, I don't want to be wasting time wondering what to do because I don't have recipes on hand."

"They're secret." Her expression said she wasn't messing around.

He nodded, gravely. "Your secret's safe with me, ma'am."

Crystal appeared with coffee for both of them, the delicious scent of vanilla mingling with the spiced aroma of heated molasses. Danny drew a deep breath of appreciation that made Meg laugh. "Doesn't that smell just pull you in?"

"I can't imagine why you don't weigh considerably more than you do," he told her, as he wheeled out the flour and sugar bins. "I expect you're good at skipping meals."

"Around here, two cookies *is* a meal," Crystal informed him. "Flour, eggs, butter. Why, it's almost a pancake. Right, Meg?" She flashed wide-eyed innocence his way before turning to Meg for confirmation.

"Exactly." Meg beamed agreement. "You're learning, Crystal." As Crystal headed back to the front of the store, Meg shifted right, forgetting to buttress her right arm before moving. "Ouch."

Danny moved to her side in a heartbeat, concern shading his features. "Did you bump it? Are you okay?"

"I'm fine. I just forgot it needed a little support." He bent low, putting him way too close for comfort, too close to imagine anything but gazing into those gentle gray eyes the rest of her life.

She was slated to have a rough four weeks. Returning his look, smelling the hint of morning after-shave mixed with molasses and vanilla, provided a sensory overload of the very best kind—but it was a delight she needed to avoid, right?

"You're sure?" He leaned forward, looked like he was going to kiss her, right before he shifted back, teasing. "Ground rule number one— No kissing until the work is done."

"How about no kissing at all?" she retorted, somewhat frustrated by the near kiss that turned into a total miss. "That's better yet."

"Naw, it's not, but if I start kissing you I might not want to stop and this timer says I've got four minutes to work on chocolate chip cookie dough before I take the molasses cookies out of the oven. Work first."

The fact that he was right tweaked her more. Overbearing and bossy, that's what he was. But she was having fun nevertheless.

That should have scared her, but instead it enchanted her.

She talked him through the recipe step by step. He fumbled a little but seemed to have found his rhythm by the time they got to Snickerdoodles later in the day.

"My grandma makes these," he told her, as he swiped crumbs from his mouth and sleeve before helping himself to another sample. "But yours are better. Consider this dessert," he announced, inspiring Meg's smile.

He'd ordered a pizza delivered, knowing Meg's parents would be along soon. Danny knew that once the family descended, these hours alone with Meg, of helping her, laughing with her, caring for her would be done for the day, but he had a month in front of him. Four short weeks to see if he had what it took to be the man worthy of her love. Some moments he felt sure, others...not so much.

But the warmth blossoming inside him felt stronger now than it had that morning or the day previous.

He would not hurt her.

Watching as she gave Crystal instructions on how to balance the register, he prayed he was right. Her small but tough demeanor thinned in personal relationships. He recognized that. And he didn't want to tip the scales until he was sure enough of himself that he wouldn't let her down.

He was leaving.

She was staying.

That couldn't be forgotten, but in this day and age, would it matter that much?

Can you dump more on Mary Clare than she's handling now? Is that fair? Or wise?

That question put the brakes on his plans. Mary Clare shouldn't be thrust into more than she could handle. He was fully aware of the delicate balance she maintained these days.

The fear of man brings a snare, but whomever trusts in the Lord shall be safe.

The quote from the book of Proverbs tweaked him. He'd grown so accustomed to being the go-to guy that he'd let his trust in God slide years before. Right now, with Meg's injury and Mary Clare's moment of testing, he realized the fruitlessness of his control.

Let go and let God.

Grandma's words bathed him with hope and peace, her matter-of-fact air a delight.

Meg lifted her gaze just then, saw him watching. She studied his face. Wondering. Maybe reading his mind. Not like it was all that difficult at this moment. He was falling for her, head over heels.

You love her.

He recognized the feeling, the punch-to-the-gut, how-did-I-get-here spasm that couldn't be denied, an internal wake-up call.

He loved her.

He *must* love her, because he was wearing a calico apron.

A commotion of voices severed the moment as Hannah and Meg's family pulled up around back. Danny surveyed the kitchen, satisfied with his efforts.

He'd helped, he'd listened, he'd learned and he'd promised himself one kiss at the end, just one. Now that the troops had arrived, he'd be saving the promised kiss for later.

Chapter Fourteen

"Danny intends to help you?" Adam Russo waved toward the apartment above them once Danny had said good-night. "Even though he's the competition?"

Meg glanced around her small store, a mock-sage expression teasing her father. "Looking for insider secrets, no doubt."

"It's not that I'm concerned," Adam began. "But I don't want you hurt. Again."

"Life doesn't come with guarantees, Adam."

Adam directed a steady gaze toward Karen. "I know that."

"And remember how we felt when we learned about Ben's condition?"

His face softened. "Yes."

"And other than his current stint of willfulness, that came out just fine. We've made great friends we'd never have met otherwise, we've raised him to be as self-sufficient as we could and he's possibly about to start a whole new adventure in life."

Meg kept her voice soft, knowing Ben might overhear. "Such as?"

"In His Care, the adult-care facility just outside of Wellsville has a job opening."

Meg frowned, not understanding.

"They need an evening dishwasher. Since Ben's at The Edge five days a week for lunches, this would give him additional work hours, more money and keep him busy in an independent setting."

"How's that?"

Karen slipped into the chair alongside Meg and sighed. "He'd be living there."

"Really?" Meg didn't try to minimize the joy in her voice. "Mom. You caved?"

"Not yet, but she will." Adam settled into the chair on Karen's other side and grasped her hand. "It's less than fifteen minutes from us, he'd have his own one-bedroom suite, access to the dining area whenever he wanted or he can cook simple things in his kitchenette."

"And he's fully capable of that," Meg noted.

"Their van is available to take him back and forth to The Edge, he'd be a participating and independent member of an adult community and they provide transportation to the stores in Wellsville twice a week so residents can shop, see a movie, go out to eat."

"It sounds ideal."

"Theoretically." Karen drew a deep breath and whooshed it out. "We've got a few days to make the decision, but Dad and I talked with the social worker, and she told us what we already knew. Ben's mature, he's a little bored and he needs to feel like he's an integral part of society while following society's rules."

"And if it doesn't work out, he can always come home," Adam added with a squeeze to Karen's hand. "But if we don't allow his independence soon, we might miss the window of opportunity because Ben sticks his feet in the mud easily."

"A quality he gets from you, dear." Karen returned Adam's squeeze with a shoulder nudge. "In any case, I'm praying about it, but I agree, it's probably for the best and we can always change the decision. We're going to have Ben tour the facility, meet people, see the kitchen and the apartment. Gauge his reaction."

"That's a great idea."

Karen's gaze sharpened. "You're exhausted."

"No, I'm—"

Karen stood, drew Adam up beside her and raised a hand. "I've been your mother long enough to know the signs, Megan Marie. We're leaving. You go to sleep. And if you miss the Fourth of July services tomorrow, we'll let Reverend Hannity know why."

"Thank you." Earlier Meg hadn't felt too bad, but right now a mix of fatigue and dull, throbbing pain worked its way from her arm to her head.

"You're all right? Really?" Her mother's gaze

meant *are you all right* in every way possible under the sun; the arm, the head, the cute guy next door…

Meg nodded and shrugged. "I'm fine. Just beat."

"Okay." Karen hugged her carefully. "We love you, honey. And we'll muster up man hours to help with whatever needs doing. You know that."

Meg did know that, but her parents both worked full-time jobs. It was a rough economy out there, where no one in their right mind took time off unless absolutely necessary, and they had a special-needs son facing a monumental change. "Between Hannah, Crystal, you guys and Danny, we'll do just fine."

"We will." Adam leaned down and kissed her brow, his fatherly affection enough to mist Meg's eyes. Adam Russo was a great man, the kind of guy every girl should find at some point. Strong, gentle, funny, faithful.

Was her mother just lucky or had there been a clue years back, something that told her Adam was the right choice?

Meg was too tired and sore to ferret out an answer. She thought the pain in her arm and head would keep her awake, but it didn't. She fell asleep once her head touched the pillow, and she didn't awaken for over seven hours.

Her head felt better, her arm didn't, but her brain seemed sharper than the previous night, which meant the reality of facing the next few weeks of busy festival time with a broken arm broadsided her.

But Danny would be there to help.

Anticipation trumped pain, and Meg didn't make light of that. Thoughts of seeing him, working with him, laughing with him...

She'd missed the promised kiss last night, her family out-staying her cute tenant, but she hoped to make up for it today. Too much caution could be as bad as too little. They had four weeks together, a decent amount of time to test the waters.

People drown in those waters, Meg.

Meg shushed the voice. She was old enough and smart enough to make her own decisions, forge her own path.

So she'd made mistakes. Who didn't? She refused to listen to her inner doubts anymore. She'd learned her lesson the hard way. She looked forward to spending the time with Danny.

With his smile, his look, the sweet, funny, strong spirit within him.

Her phone rang, interrupting her thoughts. "Hello."

"Are you ready for church?"

Meg glanced down at her robe. "Five minutes?"

Danny laughed. "Which means you're not even close. Do you feel up to going?"

She did, actually. "Yes."

"Then I'll drive us. No sense tiring you out before a long day."

"Not so long," she told him. "The store's closed

for the Fourth of July, and the girls are doing the cookie and fudge booths at the festival."

"I meant for the fireworks tonight. I hear they're spectacular."

Meg knew a guy like Danny had probably enjoyed fireworks all around the world. "They're really nice."

"I'll be over in ten minutes."

"Okay."

She headed to the closet, examined the options and sighed.

Buttons. Zippers. Pullovers with small necks not meant for easing over a splinted arm.

Tears pricked. She tamped them down, determined to figure this out. Hanger by hanger she recognized the inconveniences she'd face for the next six weeks, but it wasn't the end of the world. She settled on a gray floral wraparound skirt with a white wrap ruched top that tied at the side.

She slipped a barrette into one side of her hair. The humid temperatures added a layer of frizz to her curls.

Wonderful.

She was late, sweaty, with no time for makeup, and her hair resembled a badly trimmed bush. What normal, great-looking All-American guy wouldn't fall for that? She swung the lower door open with her left arm and found Danny, hand raised, ready to ring the bell. "I'm ready."

His grin disarmed her as appreciation lit his eyes. Suddenly she knew the clothes and hair didn't matter.

"You look wonderful."

She flushed, but refused to argue the point. "Thank you. Can you tie this for me, please?" She held out the white cotton ribbon. "I tried but couldn't even manage a decent square knot."

"Got it." He bent slightly and tied a halfway decent bow, his big fingers surprisingly nimble. "There you go."

"Thank you."

"You're welcome." He leaned down and met her mouth with his, a soft kiss that stirred Meg's heart. He paused, sighed, dropped his forehead to hers and breathed deep. "That's the kiss we missed last night. You owed me."

She smiled, loving the moment, the words, the teasing note in his voice. Yes, she could welcome being teased by that voice for decades to come, a thought that inspired hope and fear.

Do not be afraid for I am with you. Sure, she'd messed up before. She knew that. But she'd survived and proved she could withstand whatever came her way. Life offered chances, some good, some bad. Her parents proved that in their lives, their love, their acceptance of Ben as their child and God's child. She swallowed a sweet sigh of contentment and angled a smile up at Danny. "So…am I marked paid in full?"

He grinned, tapped her nose and reached for her left hand as he started down the walk. "Not even close."

"You're walking too fast."

"You're walking too slow. It's your arm that's hurt, not your legs, and we're late. Hurry up."

"You—"

He turned, swept the car door open with a chauffeurlike flourish, ignored her playful, scathing look and rounded the hood in record time once she was in. "If I speed through the village..."

"Which you won't because the sheriff's office sends Blair Carmichael to direct traffic in and out of the church circle when there are services."

"It might be worth the ticket to get to church on time."

Meg swept him a scolding look. "Nothing's worth a ticket, Danny. Waste not, want not. Take care of the pennies, the dollars will come."

"My grandmother says the same thing. She got it from her mother."

"Smart women."

"Which is why you fit so nicely, Megs." He parked the car along the edge of the church drive, the lot overflowing with Independence Day churchgoers, a sweet ritual intrinsic to Jamison no matter what day the Fourth fell on.

"Because I remind you of your grandmother? I'm not exactly sure how to take that."

He jogged around the car to help with her door. "In the best way possible. Sit with me today, okay?"

"You won't pester me?"

He grinned. "I can't promise that."

"Then, no."

"Megs."

"Promise." She tilted her head back and met his gaze, keeping her look adamant. "There's no messing around in church. Eyes forward. Prayerful. Attentive. Got it?"

"Oh, yeah. I've got it." He clasped her hand, ran his thumb across the soft, freckled skin along the back and squeezed lightly. "I'll behave."

"Then yes, I'll sit with you, especially since they're already singing and we're conspicuous. Pick a back pew. Please."

He led the way in, slipped into a pew toward the back, and opened a hymnbook for her. Her grateful smile made him feel bigger, stronger, all for holding a praise book politely.

He joined in the song, groping for the occasional word, his gaze forward, eyeing the congregation. Red, white and blue dominated the whitewashed room, the village of Jamison unafraid to bear the country's colors with pride. He skimmed Meg's gray and white with a wondering glance before realization struck. He'd had a rough time getting in and out of clothes with his broken arm back in high school, and men didn't have the complicated clothes that women grappled with. And Meg had no one around to help tie, adjust or zip, easing her arm through sleeves.

The tiny smudge of softness grew within him once again, warmth stealing a larger part of his heart, the need to cherish her an awakening. He sat alongside her, listening to Reverend Hannity speak of God's love among the sinners, the lost, the least, the lonely, and he reached for Meg's good hand.

She looked up, surprised and pleased.

He'd traveled Europe and parts of the Middle East. He'd gone to Africa on cacao bean inspections with cocoa buyers, investigating where to get the best Fair Trade chocolate to use for Grandma Mary's. He'd set up shops in cities great and small, and kept apartments in a couple of them. He'd dated, he'd laughed, he'd danced, he'd cried, but nothing he'd experienced in his thirty-four years felt as good and right as this simple act of holding Meg's hand in church, surrounded by sweet country folk who openly loved God and country. He'd found the heartland, right here in the Southern Tier of New York, and no matter what happened, he wasn't about to give it up.

Which meant marrying the girl. Having babies, raising children.

Would they have her curls, her fair skin, those golden-brown eyes that tugged him in? His stare drew her attention. She quirked a brow, tapped the book and sent him a look of censure, the expression reminding him he'd promised to face forward.

He would, but first he slipped his arm around her shoulder and dropped a gentle kiss to her hair, wanting her to feel what he felt, tenderness stealing into crevices left wanting for too many years.

She ducked her head against his chest for just a moment, the move saying she understood as they stood to sing a song.

The warmth stole deeper, further, trickles of light and faith tempting him to embrace a new day.

Nesting finches caroled just beyond the window, their well-built home tucked into the corner of the frame, their song vibrant with the coming day, the moment at hand.

Danny couldn't agree more.

After church, Danny handed Meg a maple twist roll, took a bite of his and nodded in excessive appreciation for Miriam Schultz's Amish brilliance. "This is fantastic. When do we get breakfast?"

Meg raised her sweet roll. "You're eating it."

"Real breakfast, Megs. Ham. Eggs. Toast. Coffee."

"Seriously? This won't do it for you?" She eyed the twist, then the guy, and shrugged. "Okay, I get it. You need guy food. Do you have food in your apartment?"

"That would require equipment and preparation knowledge, neither of which I have."

"You eat out constantly?" The idea of that seemed downright wrong and maybe totally fun. A life without cooking, without thinking of what to buy, what to eat, what to prepare?

"I'm always traveling from venue to venue, so stocking multiple kitchens and shopping hasn't made the short list. If I'm desperate for home cooking then I call a friend and beg an invitation."

Meg swept him a knowing look. "I don't expect you have to beg very hard."

He grinned and shrugged, teasing. "That depends on the friend. You don't eat out much?"

"Barely at all," she admitted. "By the time my day is done I couldn't care less what I eat before I crawl into bed. I grab a sandwich. Or scramble some eggs. Or beg off Mom and Dad. But I don't cook. My domesticity stops at the baking oven and the candy counter."

"Life filled with cookies, candies and you." Danny grinned at her. "I could get used to that."

"For four weeks. And then you're leaving," she reminded him.

"M-Meggie! D-Danny! Hey, you guys!"

Meg turned. Ben's enthusiasm was contagious. "Hey, Ben. How're you doing?"

"Ben, my friend, good morning." Danny clasped Ben's hand with all the gentility of the executive he was, meeting Ben's gaze, his smile and his somewhat questionable hands without a glimmer of hesitation.

Meg could have fallen in love right there. Danny's integrity shined through his acceptance of the disabled young man. "Are you hungry? I've got maple twists here."

"Mom made breakfast," Ben explained, then waved an arm across the park round to the general area of their parents. "W-we're waiting for traffic to clear a little. Just a little."

Meg smiled. "Us, too."

"You didn't walk?" Ben frowned as though surprised, then slapped a hand to his head. "I forgot you broke your arm, Meggie! How is it today, is it okay? Are you feeling better?"

"Much." Meg slipped her good arm around her brother's waist and hugged him. "And thanks for asking. Yes, Danny drove and then we're heading to the festival. Mom said she's bringing you to the fireworks tonight?"

"Yes, I love fireworks now, don't I, Meggie? When I was a little kid—" he shifted Danny's way, his gaze sincere and innocent "—I used to be afraid but Meggie made me go. She'd say, 'Ben Russo, Russos aren't whiny-pants, we're not afraid of anything, and you're going. Fireworks are fun.' So I went—" he leaned forward as though confiding in Danny "—but I was still scared. For a while. Then I grew up."

"Meg is bossy."

Ben nodded. "Yes, she is."

"Hey." Meg eyed the two of them. "First, Benjamin, it was good for you to get used to them and I did you a big favor." She swung her attention back to Danny and arched a brow of candor. "And you keep your opinions to yourself. I'm not the least bit bossy."

"Hey, guys." Hannah paused the loaded van opposite them, swept the trio and the traffic a glance as she waited her turn to progress around the circle. "Is Meg bossing you guys around?"

"Yes."

"Yes."

"No." Meg fixed the two men with a steel-eyed look, then crossed to the van while Hannah waited for Blair to give her the okay sign to move. With the round park configuration, and the five churches facing the round, access to I-86 sometimes took long minutes if you wandered through the village at the wrong time. Like now. "You're all set?"

"Yup. I've got everything on board for both booths."

"Thanks, Hannah. I know I said I'd do it, but—"

Hannah flashed her immobilized arm a look of sympathy. "Just remember I'm more available in the summer and be glad it happened now. If it had to happen at all," she added. "But…" She leaned closer, one eye on the traffic cop, and directed her words to Meg. "This opens a great window of opportunity, if you get my drift. For those smart enough—"

"Brave enough," Meg corrected.

Hannah acknowledged that with a frank smile. "And brave enough to take it. You're guaranteed to miss one hundred percent of the chances you don't take, Meg."

"Except I've already missed one hundred percent of the ones I *did* take. A lousy batting average," Meg said.

The deputy raised a beckoning hand toward Hannah. She nodded and released the brake. "Whenever God closes a door..."

"I get it, I get it. But generally when I open windows, all I get is bugs."

"Cynical." Hannah smiled at Danny, winked at Meg and eased forward. "And just when I thought you were beginning to soften up."

Meg backed away from the van, considering Hannah's words.

She *had* gotten cynical, and it wasn't exactly a stellar quality. But changing those inner doubts, those cast-out feelings? That task proved much tougher than she'd thought.

Danny's smile tugged her toward him. A huge part of her wanted to resist. She knew he was temporary, and she'd been twice burned.

But another part of her yearned for the romance, the kindliness and steadfastness she read in his gaze, his smile. Try as she might, she couldn't move fully forward or fully back, and the indecision weighed heavy on her soul.

A normal girl would have just gone for the ride, summer romance or not, to see what might develop.

Caution dictated she couldn't do that, but longing pushed her forward, caught like the nice-looking sheriff's deputy behind her, directing traffic around him while stuck immobile in the middle.

Danny reached for her hand once she stepped onto the boardwalk. "I think we'll be clear enough to get out if we head back to the car now."

"You're right." She smiled up at him.

He leaned closer. "You okay?"

"Fine."

"Ah. Fine." He nodded as if that one word held all the answers. "Gotcha."

Ben headed back toward the park with them. "I'll s-see you later, okay, guys?"

"Yes." Meg gave him a true smile, knowing big changes might be in store for her little brother and wondering how he'd handle them.

In God's hands. In His time.

She knew that. Believed it. Why on Earth did she have such a hard time living it? Why did she always need to force God's hand?

"Whatever has you looking that serious needs to stop right now." Danny halted their progress, turned her to face him and raised her chin. "It's the Fourth of July, we've got a glorious day, and unless it's your arm bothering you, you need to relax. Stop anticipating the next wrong turn."

"And if I'm looking at him?"

He scratched his jaw, winked and smiled. "And if you're not?"

"I'm being a jerk, aren't I?"

"Kind of. But you're still cute, so I'm willing to chance it."

Meg scanned the green, the crowd thinning as people hurried off to picnics, barbecues and festivals held to honor the day. "Then I'm done worrying. And whining."

"You haven't whined. But the worrying does need to stop. We take this one day at a time, got it? I'm still hungry, and there's a great festival a few minutes away. I say we change into comfortable clothes and head over, all right?"

"Okay."

He opened the car door, watched as she maneuvered the shoulder belt into place with her left hand. "I could have helped."

"I've got six weeks of fumbling, which means six weeks to get good at all this. But thanks."

"You're welcome, Miss Stubborn."

Danny climbed into the driver's seat, fastened his belt and started the engine before looking her way. "Tenacity is what's kept you building your business, step by step, layer by layer. The stubbornness?" He made a face. "That could get us both in trouble." He eased the car around and headed back out the church driveway. "But I'm a Romesser and a Graham, Megs, Irish and German. We wrote the book on trouble."

"Which means?"

"In baseball terms, I'll go whatever way the ball curves and in the end, I'll make the play as needed."

"Did you just compare me to a baseball game? Are you really that cocky?"

He grinned. "I prefer self-assured, but yes. I am. Most of the time." He flexed his shoulder muscles for her benefit, then smiled when she laughed. "And when I'm not, I pretend I am because victory never goes to the weak."

And that was what scared Meg the most. Not that he was self-assured; she admired that quality. But his natural ability to pretend, to play a part, to be someone he wasn't…

That scared her no end.

Chapter Fifteen

"I love festival games," Meg admitted as they walked among rows of crafters and artists, patriotic-draped booths tempting the palate and the wallet. "Let's throw darts at the balloons, okay?"

For just a moment Danny thought she was kidding. His phone vibrated, pulling his attention. He pulled it out in case it was Mary Clare, saw a text that said some of his buddies had rented a beach place in the Hamptons for the holiday weekend, and glanced around, his life suddenly completely different from what had been the norm a short year ago.

"Darts?" He noted her frown and glanced at her broken arm. "Left-handed?"

"No. You'll shoot. I'll watch. Very manly." She tugged him forward, but nodded to the phone he still held. "Was that important?"

"Not in the least." Looking at her, he realized the truth of his statement. Being here with her had taken on a greater measure of importance—and missing a weekend with the guys in East Hampton?

Inconsequential.

He repocketed the phone and followed Meg to a charity booth set near amazing varieties of fried foods. His rumbling stomach made everything seem enticing. But first...

He stepped up to the dart booth and offered Meg a gentleman's bow. "Allow me, fair lady."

Meg sighed, knowing they were the talk of the town already. "Could we make at least a small attempt at being inconspicuous? Please?"

"This coming from the woman who dresses in nineteenth-century gowns most days?" Danny grinned, paid the man for five darts, took aim and tossed lightly, hitting and breaking two balloons. He turned back her way. "I don't do inconspicuous, Megs."

"I see that. But that's okay because I get to pick a prize, right?"

"It would be ungentlemanly to suggest otherwise. Your choice, my lady."

Meg pointed to a brown-and-white stuffed puppy. "I'd like him, please."

The man handed the stuffed animal over, then expressed his thanks when Danny slipped him a generous donation to the charitable foundation. Meg smiled up at Danny, clutching her dog. "That was a nice thing to do."

"No big deal. And you noticed I showed off my skill first."

She grinned. "I did notice that, He-Man. And we're heading toward food, I see. Again."

"Fried vegetable medley. With ranch dressing for dipping."

"And fried Twinkies. And Oreos."

Danny veered left suddenly, pulling her with him. "Oops. This way first."

Meg followed, then laughed outright. "Of course, if you're from Buffalo, the chicken wing booth is the draw of the day."

"Just remember that a nationwide tradition started on the streets of Buffalo. There isn't a restaurant or sports bar that doesn't try to pretend they do the best wings around. But here—" Danny waved a hand toward the oversize banner hanging above the booth before them "—is the real thing, a restaurant destined to be named to the Chicken Wing Hall of Flame at some point. I am a happy man."

"Oh, brother."

Danny raised a hand. "I get that this will be tricky for you one-handed, but Megs…" He drew her forward, his teasing smile saying he knew best. "You're about to fall in love. With food," he added, the smile turning into a grin.

"Food's good," she told him, matching his smile, her left hand feeling right and perfect sandwiched in his. "And don't they make boneless wings now? For us manually challenged people?"

"We do." The woman behind the counter flashed a look of sympathy toward Meg's arm sling. "And we have breaded or uncoated."

"Breaded," Meg decided.

Danny pretended outrage. "Breaded? Boneless? That's not even close to the real thing, Megs."

She dropped her gaze to her bad arm before drawing it back to Danny. "Right now easy sounds good."

Sympathy flooded him, right up until he realized he was being played. "How long are you going to need babying?"

She dimpled. "Several more long weeks."

"Great." He paid for their order, dropped an arm around her shoulders and gave her a gentle squeeze, mindful of her injury. "And then I'm taking you up to Buffalo for wings. The real deal. Maybe we'll be able to head up there for the Chicken Wing Festival in September."

Meg slanted her gaze to his. "I'd like that."

He would, too. He paused, then nodded toward a gracious brick building centered on a hillside overlooking the festival field. "What's that?"

Meg turned. "The Reese School. It was a private school for young ladies of good breeding back in the day. Now it's the town museum."

"Is it still open?"

She nodded. "They keep it open during the festival so people can browse. It's nice. Peaceful. Our link with the past. There are walls of photos of old-timers and buildings that have been destroyed. And there's clothing, artifacts, farm implements. All kinds of things. Would you like to see it?" She swept the festival a look. "This will all be here later if you'd like to see the museum before it gets dark."

Danny generally ran from anything with the word *museum* in it, but getting to know Meg meant getting to know her roots. Her love of history was part of that. "I'd like that."

"Good."

The wing woman drew their attention. Danny accepted their order and led the way to a group of picnic tables in a shaded grove. By the time they were done, the early-evening temps had soared into the upper eighties.

Meg pointed out the trees surrounding the museum as they approached. "They kept this well-forested because of the young ladies' delicate compositions."

"Seriously?"

She grinned. "Yes. We delicate flowers must be shaded, don't you know?"

"Right." He sent her a look of disbelief as they stepped into the school's foyer. History surrounded him; the old-wood, dusty scents and sights of things long past were something he generally avoided, but not today. Not with Meg. "Will it be too warm in here for you?" He glanced at her arm. "Injuries sometimes mess up your internal temperature control."

"I'm fine." She moved forward, her look and bearing a testimonial to the respect she offered the past. Danny followed along, scanning artifacts and photos that had been carefully pieced together from attic remnants. He paused at one blown-up picture and called Meg's attention to it. "Is this the same festival, way back then? Or a different one?"

Meg stepped back. She furrowed her brow, studied the picture, and then tapped a small, crimped note beneath it. "Independence Day Picnic, 1938. Same festival. Different name."

Danny started to step back, when his eye caught something in the picture. "Meg."

She swung back. "Hmm?"

"Look at this." He pointed to a booth at the back of the picture, a stenciled sign above an apron-clad woman, a smile on her face, her hair pinned up in an old-fashioned style. "Do you see that name?"

Meg grinned. "Mary Sandoval's Candies."

Danny's heart gripped. He leaned closer, peering into the glass as if doing so might make her image brighter. Clearer. "That might be my great-grandmother."

"You don't recognize her?"

He pointed out the date. "There was no money for pictures back then. They'd just made it through the Depression, and it was right before we got into the war. Great-Grandpa fought in World War II, and when he got back they moved to Buffalo with my grandmother. He got a job at Bethlehem Steel, and Great-Grandma became friends with a Greek candy maker who gave her his supplies when he got too sick to work. And that gift was what launched Grandma Mary's success. We've got older pictures, but none from when she was younger. The few they had burned in an apartment fire in the late forties."

He touched a reverent hand to the frame. "I wonder if I could get a copy of this? My grandmother would love it."

"We'll ask." Meg motioned toward a woman upstairs. "That's Janet Ernst, the town historian. She might even have more information about your family."

"Sandoval…" The museum director pursed her lips, then worked her jaw. "When old Ike Thomas passed on, his kids brought me a trunk of old photos from the Thomasville settlement along Route 19. It never really developed into anything other than a collection of old buildings, all gone now. Development followed the water and the rails, and Thomasville was just a touch north and south of anything that meant much. But I'll look through that trunk, see if I find anything."

"Thanks, Janet."

"Yes, thank you." Danny indicated the framed newspaper clipping on the adjacent wall with a glance. "And is there a way we can copy that? For my grandmother?"

Janet studied the print, obviously reluctant, then shrugged. "Let me consider it. I don't want anything happening to the posting—paper artifacts are quite delicate, you see..."

Danny wasn't sure what she thought might happen with today's instant technology, and he knew that good photographers could actually sharpen the aged images with computerized photographic copiers, but he kept silent, allowing her time.

"How about if I have a photographer contact you," he said finally, bridging the impasse. "She can explain the procedure and you can decide if it's safe enough." He took a half step forward, then waved a hand toward the picture. "If that is my great-grandmother tending her Independence Day booth, it would be a wonderful thing to have in the family. Our photos of her were all lost in a fire, so anything you might have here is our family legacy."

She caved, just like Danny had hoped she would. "Have your photographer contact me. I'm sure we can arrange something. In the meantime, I'll check out that trunk, see if there are any other old photos from that time period. It's nice for us to note your great-grandmother's success, especially with you back in town." Her firm handshake made Danny feel like he'd passed a time-honored test, like he belonged.

"Thank you." As Meg led the way out of the old school, Danny thought about the picture, the past, the present.

"It's weird, isn't it?" he asked Meg as they walked down the long stairway leading back toward the village green. "That place. My great-grandmother's booth, her picture."

"It's history, Danny." Meg gave the small town a fond glance. "That's why it fascinates me. How all the tumblers have to click into place just so for us to be where we are, when we are, who we are."

"Or it just happens and we need to explore underlying reasons because we're innately curious beings."

Meg shook her head, watching folks wind through the red, white and blue of the festival booths and tents, American pride showcasing the day. "I've never believed that, despite my mess ups. I believe every day has a purpose, every flower has a season, every moment has potential. If I didn't believe that, why would I get out of bed every morning?"

"Necessity? Need?" He plucked a wildflower and tucked it behind her ear, then smiled at the whimsy of his act. "What if some things just are, Megs?"

She sank onto a park bench outside the museum and motioned toward the throng of people across the way. "Some place over there is my brother, Ben."

Danny nodded.

Meg studied the grounds, then turned Danny's way, her face serene despite the heat and her arm, neither of which could be very comfortable at the moment. "Ben's condition affects everything we do. Our choices. Our days. As his family, we've had to take on extra to provide properly for him."

Danny sat down next to her. "Like my uncle Jerry."

Meg watched him, waiting.

"Uncle Jerry was my mother's brother and my best friend growing up." He saw Meg's look of puzzlement, and settled back on the bench more fully. "He had a mild case of cerebral palsy and the heart and mind of a six-year-old, but that made him the perfect playmate for me. Until I grew up and moved away. Then I barely saw him." He didn't try to mask the hint of regret that rode roughshod on that memory.

Meg laid her hand atop his. "I wondered why you were so good with Ben."

Danny shrugged. "Jerry died while I was moving up in the world of corporate candy."

"Doing your job."

"Well, yes." Danny frowned, her words simplistic. "I was doing my job, but I could have—"

"We know not the day or the hour," Meg quoted Matthew's gospel. She gave Danny's hand a light squeeze. "Your regret is normal, but there are always unanswered questions or regrets when God calls someone home."

Meg's words reflected Grandma's opinion, how she'd told Danny much the same thing. "Your experience with your uncle has made you a better person," Meg went on. "I see that every time you're with Ben, the way you treat him. The way you bought the fruit and gave it to a food pantry. I think you do your uncle Jerry proud every single day, Danny."

Her words buoyed him. Dark was beginning to settle. Danny stole an arm around her and tugged her closer. "Should we head over for the fireworks?"

Meg shook her head. "We're in a great spot. We might miss a couple of the ground displays, but a lot of people will watch from the hill."

The crowd proved her right as cool night descended. People wandered up the slope, settling into lawn chairs, onto blankets, watching and anticipating the show, and at the first volley of bright-toned whistlers, Danny settled back, peaceful.

Whispered words, light laughter and the occasional voice of a child surrounded him, but his awareness was filled with the rightness of being here, his arm curved around Meg, the scent of her hair a blend of sweet and spice along his chin. He wondered if Great-Grandma had sat on this same rise, watching fireworks with his grandmother, telling her stories, feeding her homemade candy.

His mother had sent Mary Clare to the big cities to help spread her wings, give her strength, despite the reluctance he and his father shared. Then she'd plunked him into Allegany County to help him find roots. A few weeks ago he'd have laughed at the idea of faith and family, but he wasn't laughing now, not with Meg's sweet warmth curled next to him, her appreciation of the day contagious.

He dropped a light kiss to her hair.

She glanced up, puzzled, but smiling.

He couldn't find words to say what he felt, not right then, but she read his look and her smile deepened.

Then and there he decided he wanted a lifetime of those smiles, despite the challenging logistics of his job and her family. There had to be an intelligent way to work this all out.

Mary Clare's plight came back to him, the breached security in Philadelphia, her concerns about safety. He'd promised his help to her, a promise he'd never break, understanding her fragile and emotional mental state. Grief didn't follow prescribed time lines, and his sister meant the world to him now that he was old enough to appreciate her and not torment her with teasing.

But he'd promised Meg the same thing.

He could only hope and pray the two worlds didn't collide.

Let go and let God...

That didn't seem quite so easy in real life, and Danny was a man of his word. Hopefully, he wouldn't be put to the test anytime soon.

Chapter Sixteen

"Megs, are you crying?" Danny crossed the candy store floor in quick steps a few days later, then crouched by her side, concerned. "Hey."

Meg frowned and pouted, chagrined to be caught in an emotional meltdown. "I thought you were gone."

"I was. I'm back. What's wrong? Is it your arm? Does it hurt? It really shouldn't at this point."

He'd been the first to sign her cranberry-toned cast, positioning his name carefully so every time she glanced down a little heart with 'DANNY' in it looked back at her. "My arm's fine. It's Ben."

"Ben?" Danny took a seat beside her, picked up her hand and waited, his gaze concerned. "What's wrong with Ben?"

"My parents took him to see the adult living facility today. They have a job opening there. Ben could work a few nights a week washing dishes in the kitchen, and he'd have his own little apartment."

"It sounds ideal."

"To us, maybe," Meg agreed. "He burst into tears at the very thought of moving there, promised to be good, dropped onto his knees begging my parents not to send him away, and had Mom and Dad in tears alongside him."

Danny gripped her fingers tighter. "Oh, Meg. I'm sorry."

She shook her head and withdrew her hand, grabbed a handful of tissues and blew her nose. "It probably sounds dumb—"

"Not in the least."

She shot him a grateful look. "I don't know if we've sheltered him too much or let him believe he was more capable than we should have. He craves independence but he's scared to take that leap."

"Were you scared on your first day of kindergarten?"

"Petrified." She widened her eyes, nodded, and dabbed her face with fresh tissues. "I sobbed as the bus pulled away from our house, and I pressed my face against the window so my parents could see just how unhappy I was."

Danny grinned. "I'll keep that image with me always. And when you got to school it was okay?"

"After the first hour I'd pretty much forgotten I had a home and joined the league of happy schoolchildren forevermore."

"And Ben's cognitive level is?"

"About that of a seven-year-old." She nodded and retook his hand in a move so natural she almost didn't realize she did it. Almost. "I get what you're saying. Once he's there and enjoying his independence, he'll be fine."

"And if he's not?"

"We can bring him home."

Danny smoothed loose tendrils of hair away from her chin, her eyes. "It's hard to give people like Ben the wings they need to fly solo. Real hard. But you guys have done it. Now he just needs a little shove out of the nest."

"Easier said than done."

"Not if we move him in." Danny hiked a brow of invitation. "You and me, leaving your parents out of the mix. That way they have a degree of separation from the whole thing, then they can show up and do something with him once he's set without the excessive guilt of the move."

"You'd do that with me?"

He gave her a look that said she was being ridiculous. "I'd be glad to. And I want to talk to your parents about getting Ben to the Bronx for a Yankees game. Do you think they'd be okay with that?"

His kindness curled around Meg's heart. Offering to take Ben downstate… That meant he'd be around awhile, right?

She worked to push back the blossoming hope his words inspired. "Just Ben?"

He grinned and tapped her lightly on the nose. "I might be able to scrounge a third ticket."

She sat up straighter. "Really? I haven't been to New York City since my senior year in high school."

"A lot's changed since then, Megs. We've got motorcars and streetlights now."

Meg smiled. "Ha-ha."

He gave the front of the store a measured look. "Aren't we supposed to be doing something?"

Two cars pulled into the parking lot simultaneously. Meg nodded and stood, wishing she had historic clothes to fit with a cast but unwilling to ruin her costume dresses for the next six weeks. By mid-August the cast would be a thing of the past.

The same could be said about Danny, but she refused to linger on that thought. He had said they would take this day by day. A small part of her wondered which Danny offered the advice: the earnest businessman, the big-city-savvy single guy, the funny guy whose humor would get him applause in a comedy club or the sweet guy next door, always willing to lend a hand.

Meg hoped for the last, but she wasn't willing to discount the first three, and with a twenty-five percent chance of being right, it wasn't nearly good enough to risk her heart again. So why did it *feel* good enough? That was the question of the hour.

Who said life in a small town was quiet? Dull? Danny hadn't slept past 5:00 a.m. in over a week.

He'd baked, brewed, honeycombed, jelled and tempered time-honored recipes in Meg's quaint kitchen and loved every minute of it.

And when he'd finished that, he'd closed on Grandma's long-awaited store, lined up a local fine carpenter, Cameron Calhoun, to do the much-needed store makeover and made the McGees very happy with a generous check that would cushion their retirement nicely. Now he was moving furniture into a one-bedroom flat on the first floor of In His Care.

Danny eased his end of Ben's mattress through the bedroom door and helped Ben angle it atop the box spring. "Done."

"Great." Meg withdrew clean linens from a box to their left and handed an end to Ben. "After Danny adjusts the egg crate pad, we'll stretch this over it."

"Meggie, I make my own bed all the time." Ben sent her a peevish look, his tone disgruntled.

"Would you prefer doing this yourself, Benjamin?"

The scowl deepened before he sighed. "No."

"Then change your attitude. I think you're going to love it here. You've already met three of your old school friends, and you've been whining about getting a place of your own for two years. Now you've got it and you're going to act like a big baby?"

"I'm not a baby."

She softened her stance, her tone and her gaze. "I know that, but you need to regain some self-control.

You're a man now, not a little boy, and if you want people to treat you like a man, you need to act like one."

He sighed and bit his lower lip. "I know."

"Good. Now grab your end and let's get this done. I'm starving."

"We're h-having meat loaf tonight." Ben's frown returned. "I don't like meat loaf."

"Then we'll fix something here." Meg thrust her good shoulder toward the small kitchenette outside the bedroom door. "You've got food, stuff that's easy to fix. Stop being a pain."

"Or we could eat out." Danny threw out the suggestion as he centered the foam mattress topper into place, then reached for the upper corner of the mattress pad. "My treat."

"Could we? Really?" Ben's face lit up, the grimace erased.

"If it's okay with your sister." Danny met Meg's gaze and hiked a brow. "What do you think, Megs?"

"I think it's a great idea if Ben stops whining completely."

"Oh, I will. P-promise, Meggie."

"Well, good then. We've got a deal, Danny."

He met her smile across the bed, and Meg had to pinch herself to see if this was real. Danny's help had been invaluable all week, and to be here with her now, moving Ben into his new digs, setting things up, helping Ben transition into a new part of his life? Just plain wonderful.

Danny's ingrained comfort around Ben provided its own blessing. It felt nice to have Ben accepted for who he was, a mentally challenged young man with a heart of gold and an impish streak. But they'd get that streak under control, one way or another. Danny's matter-of-fact assistance helped make that possible.

Danny seized the checklist once the bed was properly made. "Kitchen. Check."

Ben nodded, proud.

"Living room. Check."

"B-but we've got to have them get me new shades, Danny, remember?"

Danny raised a hand, nodding. "You're right, big guy. We'll give that half-a-check until we've seen the floor director about contacting maintenance."

"Th-then we can check it."

"Absolutely, my man. Bedroom?" Danny glanced around the room, appraising, then turned his attention toward Ben. "Are we missing anything you need? You've got clothes, a hamper, your furniture, the bed's made. And do you remember how to use the washers and dryers, or do you need a refresher course?"

"I'm twenty-four, Danny."

"Oh. Well. Right." Danny nodded agreement, hands up, palms out. "Then you're good."

A light of anticipation brightened Ben's features. "I'm in my own place?"

Meg angled her head, scanned the room and nodded. "So it would seem."

"Can I have parties?"

"Not loud ones."

"Quiet ones?"

"With football season coming up? I expect that's a given." Danny crossed into the living room and tapped the flatscreen TV. "You know how to use your remote?"

"Is it the same as Mom and Dad's?"

"Yes."

"Then I know how."

"Good. Then let's eat, gang. I'm famished. We've been at this for hours." Danny put one arm around Meg and the other around Ben and herded them toward the door. "And your sister had me slaving away in the kitchen all morning, getting ready for the booth at the balloon rally kick-off parade tomorrow. Does she ever sleep, Ben? Because I'm beginning to think small-town living isn't nearly as peaceful as people make out."

Meg sent him a smile as Ben checked and rechecked his door, then double-checked his key to make sure it fit the lock before he rechecked the lock one last time.

"We're good?" Danny didn't scoff at Ben's studied carefulness, or try to hurry him along.

"We're good." Ben nodded and fist-pumped the air, a victory sign of success.

"Then let's get food. And you pick the restaurant, Ben. Your choice tonight."

Meg thought she could predict Ben's choice because his penchant for chicken nuggets was a family joke, but he surprised her when he turned Danny's way. "Can we go to the Beef Haus? They've got really good fa-fajitas there."

Dismay peppered the moment for Meg. Ben's hand-to-mouth agility was challenged with loosely wrap sandwiches, but Danny clapped him on the back, nodded and led the way to the car.

She needn't have worried. Ben studied his seasoned steak wrap, then asked the waiter for a sharp knife. Instead of trying to pick up the unwieldy sandwich, he cut it into small pieces, the task laborious for his thick hands, but when all was said and done, Ben ate his dinner like the young gentleman her parents raised him to be, his table manners impeccable.

And when it was time to say goodbye later that evening, she was the one fighting tears, not Ben. An old school friend of Ben's was being dropped off at the same time.

"Ben! Are you living here now?"

"Y-yes."

"That's good! Me and Brian are on the first floor, by the training room. How about you?"

"Me, too." Ben slapped a hand to his head and turned Meg's way, dismayed to have forgotten his manners. "Jimmy, this is my sister, Meg, and my friend Danny."

Meg reached out a hand. "I remember Jim from school. You're looking good."

Jim flexed his left arm. "I stay in shape here." He redirected his attention to Ben. "You wanna train together?"

"Sure."

"Let's go."

Ben started in before realizing he hadn't said goodbye. He turned from the inside door, waved and yelled, "Goodbye, Meg and Danny! Thanks for supper!"

Meg watched him go, half proud, half irked. "That's it? No lengthy goodbyes? No tearful pleas? Not even a kiss on the cheek?"

"There." Danny kissed her cheek, tweaked her nose and gave her a gentle shove toward the car. "Get in, what are you, crazy? Do you realize how well that went? Are you seriously trying to tempt fate by lingering out here?"

"Good point."

"My specialty." He grinned and eased the car around the drop-off circle, before offering her a thumbs-up. "Well done."

She made a little face. "It feels weird."

"Change always does, right until we figure out it was the best thing we could have done and clap ourselves on the back for thinking of it."

"True."

"You want ice cream?"

"Absolutely. What made you think of that?"

"Whenever we did something cool with Uncle Jerry we topped it off with ice cream. Ben's got his back there." He jerked a thumb toward Ben's new home. "And it's not every day a guy gets to buy his best girl an ice cream when she runs an ice cream shop."

"I'm your best girl?"

"My very best. And you handled Ben perfectly, by the way. Just enough edge, just enough sympathy."

"It was hard."

Danny acknowledged that as they joined the throng of people waiting in line at an ice cream stand adjacent to Wellsville's Little League fields. "I saw that, but you manned up. Good job."

"Thank you." Meg smiled across the parking lot and waved her left hand. "The McGees are here."

Danny followed her gaze and smiled a greeting. "Nice folks."

"They're the best," Meg declared while scanning the ice cream choices. "I don't know a harder working family in the area. They stick together through thick and thin, helping others, helping the church, helping the town. Just amazing, considering their age and health issues. May I have a caramel-almond cluster in a waffle cone, please?"

"Make that two," Danny told the counter girl, as the McGees took halting steps toward their car.

The ice cream clerk handed them their cones. Meg

licked hers, sighed in appreciation and then frowned. "Jed and Kate are leaving."

"And that's bad?" Danny asked.

"They didn't come by and say hello. Chat." Meg watched their car ease out of the parking lot and onto the road. Her tone turned thoughtful. "That's not like them."

"Busy, maybe."

"Maybe." She shrugged, her attention torn. "I hope they're feeling all right."

"They might want to get home before dark," Danny suggested. "A lot of older drivers aren't comfortable driving late."

"True." Meg swung back and raised her cone toward him. "This is marvelous, by the way. Thank you for this and for all of your help with Ben today. You've gone the distance this week, and I'm sure it wasn't part of your original plan."

Danny acknowledged that with a smile. "Way better than my original plan, actually."

Meg blushed.

A zippy sixties ringtone interrupted the peaceful moment. Danny withdrew the phone and stepped away. "Gotta take this one, Megs. Be right back."

Meg nodded and grabbed a seat at a picnic table nearby. "Okay."

He paced while he talked.

Meg noted that, watching him, a part of her wondering who got him that riled up, another part thinking she might not want to know. Danny had a life completely separate from the one she knew here. His presence was sweet but temporary, a fact she tended to downplay when they were together.

Because it feels so right to be together, her conscience scolded. *But we've been here before, right? Taken this path a time or two? Why would you risk being fooled again?*

As Danny strode back her way, Meg warred with the internal scolding but didn't pretend to win the battle. Being with Danny seemed right, but she'd stopped trusting her gut in such matters, so she'd keep things sweet and simple. A guy and a girl stopping to share a summer cone together.

End of story.

"Are you okay?" she asked when he drew closer, noting his worried expression.

He considered the question, then shook his head. "My sister's run into some trouble in Philadelphia. Part of me wants to head down there and run interference for her…"

"Making her feel inept and overshadowed by your big mover-and-shaker presence," Meg cut in.

He didn't try to deny it. "Exactly. She's newer to the big-city venues and she's quite capable. It's just—"

"You don't relinquish power easily and never to a mere woman?"

He met Meg's gaze and made a face. "Seriously, get off the soapbox, would you? If my mother or grandmother heard you, they'd die laughing because they're two of the toughest, most decisive women I've ever met, which is why you remind me of them." He chucked her under the chin. "Mary Clare's been through a rough year. Her fiancé was killed in Afghanistan late last spring."

That wasn't what Meg had been expecting to hear. Surprise and sorrow tinged her voice as she reached out a hand to his arm. "Danny, I'm so sorry."

He nodded and shrugged, stress shadowing his normally relaxed features. "Us, too. Instead of a wedding, we had a funeral."

"Oh, Danny."

"Taking on the East Coast stores for the summer is good for her," he explained, "but I feel like I should be there, helping, smoothing her way, even though I know this is the best thing for her."

"Like Ben."

He mulled that, then nodded. "Exactly like Ben. You know all that stuff I sold you about pushing him out of the nest, letting him fly?"

Meg smiled. "Easier said than done, huh?"

"Exactly. My instinct is to rescue her. My mother would strangle me if I did, and my survival instinct outranks my protective side."

"I like your mother already," Meg decided. She stood and stretched her good arm. "But I'm beat, Danny. Long day."

"A good one, though."

"Yes." She smiled up at him, then stifled a yawn.

"And you remember that I'm heading to Buffalo in the morning?"

"Corporate candy awaits. Yes, I remember."

"And Hannah's coming to help?"

"Yes, again."

"Good." He winked approval, opened her car door for her, waited until she was in and then closed the door carefully, his gentleness something Meg could get used to.

He settled into the driver's seat, the steadfastness of his presence making her feel like anything was possible at this moment. Cold reality might return by morning, but this time, this night, Meg felt a resurgence of hopes and dreams she probably shouldn't let herself feel.

But she did.

Chapter Seventeen

"Is Danny gone for the whole day?" Hannah reached around Meg to procure a box of waffle cones the next morning. Moving easily, she dipped them into melted chocolate, then crushed almonds. The quiet moment provided catch-up time.

Meg nodded as she jotted things on an order pad. "He drove to Buffalo for some business thing. He'll be back tonight or tomorrow."

"He's only been here a few weeks, but it seems weird not to have him around."

"It's nice having him here."

"If by 'nice' you mean 'amazingly romantic and wonderful,' then I agree."

"Stop. Really. We're friends. Mostly."

"When you're not kissing him."

Meg paused her order and met Hannah's look. "Is it that obvious?"

"Patently. Which has tongues wagging, but this *is* Jamison, Meg. When don't tongues wag?"

"Speaking of which…" Meg jutted her chin toward the door. "This one's all you, girlfriend."

Hannah saw Jacqui approach, holding Brad Junior's hand. She nodded and slipped through the Dutch door. "Got it." She moved to the front and offered a bright smile of welcome as the door swung open. "Jacqui, hello. And you've got the little guy with you."

"Denise had a doctor's appointment in Hornell," Brad's mother replied, her tone peevish, "so I've got him for the day and I just had to get over here to grab a few things. We've got company coming in for the balloon launch, and with the kitchen not done, I'm limited on what I can personally do. Hello, Meg." She called the last out louder to draw Meg's attention.

Meg smiled and raised her spatula in greeting as she checked warming chocolate. "Good morning."

"You're busy, as usual." Jacqui's forced friendliness made Meg sigh within, but she kept her smile firmly in place.

"I've got to temper this before the weather gets too humid, so today's forecast was perfect."

"An ideal day." Jacqui nodded agreement, asked Hannah to fix a two-pound box of mixed chocolates, then eased down the counter, closer to Meg. "Did you hear about the McGees?"

"The McGees?" Meg frowned, added broken chocolate to the tempering pot, then shook her head. "I saw them both in church on Sunday and at the ice cream stand last night. They seemed fine. All things considered." She didn't add that it was unusual for Jed and Kate to not stop and chat.

"Physically, yes, I guess that's status quo." Jacqui's expression acknowledged the aged couple's limitations. "They're selling their business."

"Really?" Meg glanced up as she pondered Jacqui's news. "That's not a big surprise, though, is it? They could probably use some time off and heaven knows if anyone deserves a little R & R, it's Jed and Kate."

"And if that were the case, I'd be all for it, too, but since they got pushed out of their store because of money problems, it's one of those situations that never should have happened here." She punctuated each syllable with a firm tap on Megan's polished counter.

Sympathy welled within Meg. Jed and Kate were long-standing members of the Allegany County business community and had been members of Good Shepherd for generations. And while they were well past retirement age, Meg understood that timing and finances didn't always allow the obvious choice, and money problems kept them in business long after they should have been able to enjoy their grandkids. "I'm sorry to hear that. I'll have to get over to their going-out-of-business sale, help their bottom line."

"And that's the worst of it," Jacqui declared, her voice rising. "That Danny Graham didn't even give them time to have a going-out-of-business sale, he just went and pushed them out the door so fast that they're having an auction next week, selling everything they've got to the highest bidder so he can open a chain candy store in their place. Like that's what we need down here." She swept Meg's store a dramatic gesture. "A Grandma Mary's candy store when we have this."

Meg's heart jugged to a stop. Her hands faltered. Her brain seized.

Danny pushed the McGees out of their storefront in Wellsville? Would he do that? Could he do that?

No. Yes.

No. Danny might be a sharp businessman, but he had a heart. Didn't he?

Jacqui interrupted her rampaging musings by leaning forward and adding, "On top of that, after snooping around to see who was down on their luck, he asked people to keep it quiet, to keep a lid on the sale. I ask you, Meg, if a man's working on the up-and-up, why would he care who knew about the sale? Hmm?"

"A lot of reasons." Hannah moved left to intercept the conversation. "When a company plans a new enterprise, it makes sense to get all your facts straight before making an announcement. And we knew that Danny was looking for a storefront for Grandma Mary's, so this isn't really news, Jacqui. Not to us."

"You knew?" Jacqui nailed Meg a sharp look, then stepped back, amazed. "You knew who he was?"

Meg nodded, her gaze trained on the chocolate, refusing to let humiliation and heartbreak ruin a lovely batch of sweet, chocolatey goodness, despite latent homicidal thoughts. "Of course. It wasn't a secret."

"And still you dated him?" Jacqui's tone said that was about the stupidest thing she'd ever heard. At the moment, Meg couldn't disagree.

Wasn't this what she feared, that she'd be played for the fool in front of the whole town again? And while Jacqui wasn't the whole town, her biting words would spread like midsummer wildfire, letting the entire populace know that Danny was a low-down, big-city businessman with nothing but his bottom line at heart, and that he'd pushed a financially strapped family out of their long-standing store.

He'd gone for the weakest link in Wellsville, his Wharton-educated analytic mind-set immune to things like old-town propriety and kindness.

And she'd bought into the act.

"Then of course you knew that he chartered Reese Lawton's plane to head to Philly now that he's done his damage here."

Meg knew nothing of the kind, but the revelation shouldn't have come as a big surprise. And it shouldn't hurt like it did, but that was her own fault for jumping into uncharted waters.

Hannah approached from the side once Jacqui left with her chocolate. Meg held up a hand to ward her off. "Not now, please. It won't matter if you offer sympathy or a swift kick in the rear, I'm holding on by a thread and I've got work to do and only one arm to do it."

Hannah nodded, then raised her hands. "But I've got two good ones here and I'll work night and day to help you. You know that."

"Thanks, Hannah." Meg may have only known Hannah a few years, but they'd become full-blown friends and comrades. And while Hannah kept her past to herself, she'd jumped into this friendship with both feet, always willing to help. But this time there was no help for Meg. Again.

Danny turned off of Route 19, excited to see the now-familiar streets of Jamison, the arching bridge over McConnachy Creek, the old-style gaslights, the beckoning warmth of the quaint village. The first time he'd come to town, he'd appreciated the well-kept historical buildings, the colors and tones in keeping with the tucked-in feeling Jamison thrived on.

Now he was urged forth by the people, their quiet warmth and integrity soothing his heart, his soul. Conventional wisdom said that his sister should have drawn this gig, leaving him cruising the East Coast for the summer.

Right now he was thanking God for an unconventional mother who was also his CEO. She couldn't have possibly foreseen the delightful end result he hoped to find with Meg, but she knew her children well enough to boot them out of their comfort zones. He could only hope he had that same chutzpah with his own children someday.

Children. Meg. Home.

Visions of their future filled his head as he parked the car on his side of Meg's store. He bounded up the steps, two at a time, impatient and eager, calling her name as he pushed through the door.

"Megs? I'm back. You in here?" Danny moved toward the kitchen light at the back of the store, anticipation lightening each step. He'd spent the early part of the day talking with Eastern Region store managers, mid-day explaining Meg to his parents and grandmother, and the end of the day picking out a ring to declare his intentions. If Meg said yes, that is. But of course she would, he reasoned. She loved him, even if saying the words put her at risk. The emotion came through her movements, her gaze, her blush, her touch.

They'd figure out logistics once life calmed down after the balloon rally. Danny would never have imagined the sleepy existence he'd scoffed at could be so busy, but he'd learned a valuable lesson about small-town entrepreneurism, and that lesson procured him a priceless educational opportunity and the girl of his dreams. Not to mention a brand-new store to make his grandmother happy.

"Megs?"

She stood with her back to him, working on something, her shoulders straight, spine rigid. She turned as he drew closer, her gaze hard, eyes cold. "Two questions, Danny."

He frowned, her expression taking him aback. "What do you mean?"

"Did you really push the McGees out of the store they'd owned for over forty years?"

There's no such thing as a secret in a small town.

Danny met her gaze and splayed his hands. "Is this an inquisition, Megs?"

"Just answer the question."

He squared his shoulders, the accusation knifing his carefully laid plans. "I made them an offer and they accepted."

"You knew their financial situation was dire?"

He nodded, clenched his hands, then nodded again, slowly. "Of course. I checked."

She sent him a thin smile. "I'm sure you did. And then you asked them to keep it quiet? Right before you chartered a plane to Philadelphia for Monday?"

How had she heard about the flight he'd already cancelled because his mother had stopped just short of threatening his life if he interfered with his sister's resurgence? Once again he realized the speed of information travel in Jamison.

He sucked a breath that helped keep him from

yelling that the common sense of the situation encouraged a quiet beginning, that he wanted to be sure everything was set before letting Grandma know they were good to go. But the look on Meg's face said she saw this differently. Where he saw an opportunity to help the McGees and himself, she sensed deceit. Where he planned a step-by-step surprise for his aging grandmother, Meg saw pretense. "Yes. Why?"

She shrugged. "You went for the weakest link, Danny. You scoured the town, investigating people's businesses, their finances, and then went for the kill by targeting a sweet old couple who've never hurt anyone. They've held onto that business through ups and downs you can only imagine because you've never had to quake or quiver over business. When you're born with a company handed to you, the reality of people like Jed and Kate doesn't mean much, but that's where we differ." She stepped forward, her face pinched in anger, her tone hard, the fingers of her uninjured arm taut. "I care about people. You don't."

Her blade-sharp words cut through his new confidence.

She was partially correct. He wasn't always good at putting people first. He'd buried himself in work, in travel, in setup, his goals tangible for a young entrepreneur set on making a name for himself.

But he'd definitely done the right thing with the McGees, despite Meg's opinion. He'd gone against the bottom-line code and balanced everything he could in their favor, recognizing their disabilities and their age. But if Meg thought him capable of low, underhanded tactics, if she doubted his integrity...

The exhilarated hopes and dreams of the day dissipated on her judgmental words, her crossed arms, her angry gaze. His right hand came in contact with the small box he'd secured in his pocket, reality smacking him in the face. She didn't trust him. And there was no such thing as love without trust.

"Were you planning on saying goodbye before you duck out to Philadelphia, or just quietly disappear?"

"I—"

"Please go."

"Megs—"

"Please."

Sunlit daydreams slipped into shadowed reality. Danny's heart clenched, then stutter-stepped as he backed toward the door. "I'll move my things out in the morning."

"And I'll refund the rest of your rent."

"Perfect."

Danny walked through the door feeling like nothing had ever been more less than perfect in his life.

He went next door, climbed the steps slowly, resisted the urge to hurl the beautiful ring against the wall in frustration and tried to lose himself in sleep, but rest eluded him. Well before dawn he packed his belongings, filled the trunk of the rental, and slipped the apartment key under Meg's door before he headed south on Route 19, the scant miles between Jamison and Wellsville not nearly enough to buffer his twisted emotions. Right now, Danny was pretty sure no amount of distance would be enough.

Chapter Eighteen

"You kicked him out?" Karen Russo stared at Meg as if she'd sprouted two heads the following evening. "Why?"

"You know the answer to that as well as I do." Meg strode across the store, pulled the blinds closed over the new Help Wanted sign she'd hung in the window, and turned off the lights. Exhaustion tugged her from all angles. She hadn't slept a wink the night before, then came downstairs this morning to find Danny's key beneath the door. No note. No goodbye. No nothin'.

Which was what she wanted, right?

"Did you give him a chance to explain?"

"He admitted everything."

"Admitted?" Karen moved closer and set her hands on Meg's shoulders. "Did you seat a jury of his peers or find him guilty on your own, Meg?"

"Mom, stop." Meg turned, tired and angry, disgusted with herself for allowing the deceit to grow out of hand and livid with Danny for being so good at what he did. "I asked. He answered. End of story."

"But is it?" Karen stepped back, waved a hand around the store and blew out a breath. "He was going to help you, remember? I can't take time off work because the other hygienist is on vacation, Dad's swamped with overtime for the first time in nearly six years and Tops is giving Crystal extra hours. How are you going to do all this on your own with a broken arm?"

"You think I should have strung him along because I needed help?" Meg shot her mother an incredulous look. "I would never do that."

"I think you should have taken time to calm down and check your facts before you went off on a nice guy who happens to be your competition. A fact you've known for a while."

"But I didn't know he was muscling people out of their businesses to feather his own nest, which is obviously why the McGees avoided us at the ice cream stand the other night."

"Establishing a store for his grandmother isn't exactly feathering his nest, Megan."

Meg wrenched the back door open, longing to slam it, wanting to slam anything right about now. She was tired, hurt and angry. Her faith in mankind had reached an all-time low and that was saying something for her, and all she wanted was…

She bit back a sigh and wanted to cry in her

mother's arms, but her mother seemed to think she was totally whacked. Well, that might be the case, but at least she was smart enough to know when to apply the brakes this time. This time *she* called the shots.

"Thanks for coming over, Mom."

Karen slipped an arm around Meg's shoulder, gave her a half hug and pressed a kiss to her cheek. "You're welcome. And try not to do too much these next few days, okay?"

The suggestion bordered impossible. Hannah had a summer reading camp going at the library, Crystal was working extra at her higher-paying job and Danny was gone, leaving Meg on her own. With a broken arm.

"I'll be fine. I always am."

Karen's look doubted Meg's assertion, but she kept her silence and left Meg alone to wrestle the hows and whys of the situation until sleep claimed her, and despite how wretchedly worn out she was, it didn't come soon enough.

Meg heard the jangle of the door the next morning and hurried from the small kitchen. She'd managed to talk the ice cream delivery guy into loading the counter freezer himself, rotating the older stock to the front. The bakery supply company did the same in the kitchen. But trying to mix, ladle, measure and scrape the big mixing bowl with her left hand was a time-consuming process, and there was no way she could make headway on such a busy week at this pace.

Still, she faced Maude McGinnity and the smaller woman accompanying her with a welcome smile as she approached the counter. Maude swept her casual clothes a look of sympathy. "Hard to get into your old-fashioned dresses with that cast, honey?"

"Impossible." Meg sent the arm a rueful look. "I didn't want to ruin the sleeves by cutting them, so people get the modern-day Meg for now."

"Which is a wonderful version, as we all know." Maude's assurance deepened Meg's smile. "Meg, this is my friend Marilyn."

"How do you do?" Meg stretched out her left hand and found the other woman's grip surprisingly strong and agile.

"Quite well, thank you. I'm in town for the summer and I saw you had a help-wanted sign posted." Bright brown eyes sparked with humor and intelligence as the gray-haired woman jutted her chin toward the window placard. "I don't know if you're looking for full-time or part-time, but I've got a lot of experience in the kitchen, and I'm good with folks in all kinds of situations. Since Maude's working all day, it seems silly for me to sit around twiddling my thumbs."

"You could help my quilters," Maude interjected.

Marilyn made a little face. "Joining a quilting team midproject is like etching your name in wet cement. No matter how good the stitching, it won't blend. But maybe this fall?" Expectant, she arched a dark gray brow Maude's way.

"You know I'd love that." Maude leaned toward Meg, almost conspiratorial. "Marilyn and I were friends in grade school, then she moved away and we didn't see each other for the longest time. But oh, the good times we had."

"Yes, we did." The smaller woman swept Meg's shop a satisfied look and sent a birdlike gaze Meg's way. "I can start right now."

"Really?" Meg faced the unexpected gift standing in front of her. "You don't mind jumping right in?"

Marilyn rubbed gleeful hands together. "No, I do not. And I understand from Maude that you've got cookie and fudge booths due this weekend for the big balloon rally."

The last thing Meg wanted to think about was the rally, because the minute it came to mind she pictured Danny in his big, bright balloon, the rainbow colors he'd described sharp against a blue summer sky.

But she wouldn't think of Danny. Not now, not ever.

Yeah, right. Good luck with that.

Meg kept her smile tight and her sighs internal. "I do, yes."

"Well I've got a knack for picking things up quick as I see them, so I think we've got ourselves a deal."

Excitement brightened the older woman's face, her steel-toned hair layered stylishly short, her dark pants offset by a deep pink golf shirt. All in all Marilyn was spritely and adorable, and if she could commandeer the counter business, Meg's one good hand could get things done in the kitchen. Meg dipped her chin in agreement and smiled. "Welcome to the Colonial Candy Kitchen."

Marilyn beamed. "It's nice to be here, honey."

A one-woman dynamo.

That's what Marilyn Schneider was, and her proficiency lifted a weight from Meg's shoulders that afternoon. Despite her age, Marilyn worked calmly, diligent and focused, those sharp brown eyes crinkled in delight. Her joy bolstered Meg's, and Meg decided then and there that God not only answered prayers, He'd sent Marilyn on purpose, knowing Meg needed someone bright, talkative and upbeat. Marilyn fit the bill.

"Oh, honey, isn't that nut cluster display just delightful?" Marilyn nodded toward the case. "And to have them all together, including the white chocolate varieties? Marketing genius, especially with the old-fashioned nut cans set off in the corner, their colors brought out by the bunting you used in front of the case. Very well done, Meg. Do they sell well?"

"Very." Meg nodded, a quiet feeling of satisfaction nudging her angst aside. They'd baked and frozen cookies to get ahead for the weekend, they'd rotated the chocolates to ensure freshness, they'd stocked paper supplies for the ice cream area, dipped cones in chocolate and rainbow sprinkles for later. And Meg was about to show Marilyn how to make fudge, another balloon rally favorite, when Marilyn's pocket began to play the opening bars of the Archie's old bubblegum hit about sugar and honey.

"Oops, I must get this. Excuse me a moment, won't you, dear?" Marilyn withdrew the phone from her side pocket, her deft hands belying her age as she paced several steps away, gladness painting her voice while Meg wondered why someone her age would use a ringtone like that.

"Yes, dear, I'm fine, just fine, having the time of my life, actually. Maude's wonderful, doing quite well in spite of our advancing years, her quilt shop's a dream come true, I could move in there tomorrow and be perfectly happy the rest of my days surrounded by plaid and calico, and it's such a joy to be back in Jamison. I've actually procured myself a job." She bestowed a warm, friendly look Meg's way, so sweet and genuine that Meg couldn't help but smile in return, and she'd been fairly certain a few hours ago she might never smile again.

At the moment, she'd meant it. Now?

Now she was beginning to realize her mother may have made a good point, that maybe, just *maybe,* she should have at least talked to Danny. Given him a chance.

But, no. She'd steamrolled him and then tossed him out on his ear.

A tiny part of her wondered where he was staying, what he was doing, but she pushed that aside as Marilyn's voice hitched up. "At the most darling candy shop I've ever seen, with a proprietor so cute and spunky she reminds me of a page in the history books, with or without her usual costuming. Well, dear, I must go. Meg's waiting to show me how to make fudge, and I'm dying to learn her secrets. Bye."

Meg nodded to the phone as Marilyn slipped it back into her pocket. "Your husband?"

Marilyn shook her head, her gaze frank. "No, Gerald died some time ago."

"I'm sorry."

Marilyn shrugged acceptance. "We had a long life together, a good life. Ups and downs, good times and bad. And we worked together," she added as she bustled into the kitchen, "so there were days when we tripped over each other and days we avoided one another, but we stayed married for over forty years before God called him home. I have no complaints."

"That's wonderful. And rare."

"Yes." Marilyn beamed. "So. Which fudge do we make first?"

Meg smiled back at her. "Your choice."

"White chocolate cherry-almond parfait."

"You've got it. Have you made fudge before, Marilyn?"

"A time or two, but not in a while."

Meg nodded understanding as she set the kettle up on her specially designed two-burner cooktop, the extrawide burners perfect for large pots, the counter set nearly a foot lower than normal to facilitate stirring. "We don't have any automated candy equipment here."

"Is automation bad?" Marilyn slanted a curious glance Meg's way.

"Not at all." Meg aligned the measuring tools and stepped back to allow more room for Marilyn. "In bigger candy stores that produce on-site they use automated stirrers, candy thermometers, timers—even self-tempered chocolate. A machine warms and tempers milk chocolate by adding chopped pieces from a hopper as needed and then paddles the chocolate to keep it glossy."

"Amazing."

"Isn't it?" Meg smiled as she handed Marilyn an apron. "But I'm small enough to do that on my own, and that helps me teach the old methods both locally and at the Genesee Country Village in Livonia."

"And while new doesn't equate with bad," Marilyn offered, her left brow thrust up in agreement, "it's good to look back and see what the past has gained for us. Or lost."

Her words of wisdom struck a chord in Meg. She

paused in her measurements, made a little face and nodded. "The past says a lot about the future, doesn't it?"

"Sometimes." Marilyn hustled around the kitchen procuring ingredients needed for the fudge. "And sometimes the past is best left alone."

"You think?"

Marilyn grinned and set the jug of light cream alongside the bin of top quality white chocolate chips. "Oh, I know. Would you like me to measure this? I'm very good at following recipe directions."

Meg gave up her spot readily. "Go for it, Marilyn, and if you have any questions, I'll be right here getting the trays ready. We won't do the chocolate varieties until Thursday, but the white chocolate holds with no loss of taste or texture. And fudge freezes well, a candy maker's best friend in the summer."

"Wonderful."

Meg smiled as she prepared two medium-size fudge trays with wide waxed paper. The day had gone much better than she'd hoped or expected. Marilyn's appearance was a dream come true, but she wasn't in a state of mind to think about dreams coming true, not with how she'd shoved Danny out the door just two days before.

She eyed her cell phone, just in case she'd missed a call. Nope. Nothing.

Biting back a sigh of indiscriminate proportions, she watched as Marilyn measured, her movements quick and lively, a tiny smile quirking her jaw as her hands seized one ingredient after another. "You're pretty good at this, actually."

Marilyn paused, offered Meg a grin, then nodded toward the pot. "I loved making fudge when my kids were small. We'd give boxes of fudge for Christmas, and we'd come up with all different kinds. They loved being part of the gift rather than just purchasing one."

"That's a great idea."

"We thought so." Marilyn leaned down, adjusted the gas flame to her satisfaction and stirred the initial mixture with Meg's big, wooden paddle. "Gifts from the heart. People should embrace that idea more than they do."

Meg couldn't agree more, but her heart wasn't in the best shape right now, for gifting or anything else. As the mixture heated, she moved back to Marilyn's side, not wanting to invade the older woman's space but needing the fudge to come out just right. Timing was a huge factor in that success, and while Meg's personal timing had been messed up lately, candy timing…well, she understood that procedure better than most.

Danny hung up the phone, paced the parking lot outside the bank, withdrew the phone, glared at it, then stuffed it back into his pocket, beyond any mere mortal level of annoyance.

Grandma was working for Meg.

Could this scenario get any worse?

No.

But he'd thought that before and things had gotten much worse, so what did he know?

He glared at the phone once again, half wanting to head north and snag Grandma out of Meg's store, half wanting to hug her for jumping in when Meg obviously needed assistance and had tossed her very willing helper to the curb.

He sighed, scrubbed the base of his neck with a hand, frowned and glanced heavenward, uncertain what to pray for, but pretty sure he could use some divine help.

"Seeking celestial intervention, Danny?"

Danny swung around at the sound of Karen Russo's voice and shrugged, bemused. "Yes, actually. Apparently your daughter has that effect on me. Hey, Ben." He reached out to shake Ben's hand, then clapped the younger man on the shoulder. "Are you loving your new crib?"

Ben laughed. "It's a-awesome. Mom's taking me to the dentist because I have o-off today, and I don't want to miss work to get my teeth cleaned."

"A good work ethic is a wonderful thing."

"I-is your balloon here yet, Danny?"

Danny shook his head. "Tonight. Have you ever gone up, Ben?" Thoughts of how Uncle Jerry clung to the ground with both feet despite Grandpa Schneider's urging pushed Danny's mind-set. "You're more than welcome to come up with me on Saturday morning. If it's okay with your mom, of course."

Karen turned Ben's way. "Adventures are always a good thing, Ben. What do you think? Would you like to go up in Danny's balloon on Saturday?"

"I would love that, Danny!" Excitement trembled Ben's speech. "M-my friends will be so jealous!"

"Ben Russo, that's not nice." Karen's frown of mild displeasure had Ben retracting his statement.

"I'll tell them maybe they can go another time."

"Much better." Karen eyed her watch, made a face of surprise and headed for the street. "Gotta go, Ben, we'll be late. Danny, what time do you want him Saturday morning?"

"By five. Launch is at 6:00 a.m."

"Five in the morning?" Surprise painted Ben's features. He clapped an exaggerated hand to his head. "That's early."

"It is." Danny cocked his head and lifted one shoulder. "Balloons launch when the wind is calm. Winds pick up during the day, so we have to launch early. You still in?"

"Yes." Ben nodded, his jaw firm, his gaze set. "I'll be there."

"Good." Danny waved to Karen, climbed into his car—his *real* car, the rental a thing of the past now that he'd completed his business deal and been outed by the locals. The well-tooled engine sprang to life. He headed toward Main Street and parked in front of the McGees' store, but Mary Clare's ringtone interrupted him. He climbed out of the car, pulled out the phone and said hello.

"Danny, you're not going to believe this."

She sounded better. Stronger. Danny leaned a hip against the car's hood and breathed a quiet sigh of relief. "What?"

"That whole drug deal? An inside job. The assistant manager was back-door-dealing us, and we got it on surveillance when he tried to cut a deal with an undercover detective from the Southwest detective bureau."

"Seriously?"

Her voice hiked up. "Joel had talked to me about the idea the other night—"

"Joel?"

"The detective from Southwest, up on Pine Street. We, um…" She hesitated, before continuing, "We went out the other night."

"Out? Like a date, out?"

"There's another kind?"

"Good point," he acknowledged. "And you talked security the whole night?"

Her light laugh inspired Danny's smile. "So it's good I cancelled my flight down there to rescue you, hmm?"

"Mom would have killed you."

Danny didn't need to affirm that their mother had made that abundantly clear. "Let's just say I saw the error of my overprotective ways. So we're all good? The bad guys are locked up behind bars?"

"Yes, and I actually stepped in to help run shift because it's important to stay connected with the store-level concerns, you know? It's too easy to get jaded if you're never in the trenches, running a store, making product, setting up displays."

Danny had learned that very same lesson himself, but it took him longer than it had his sister. Obviously his worry had been for naught, another valuable lesson learned.

Let go and let God...

"Anyway, I just wanted to bring you up-to-date and say thanks for trusting me on this. It meant a lot. Even if you did almost swoop in to take over."

Her words deepened his smile to a grin. "I'm glad it's all okay. Good job, sis."

"Thanks. Gotta go. Joel's meeting me at Smokey Joe's for lunch."

"Go. Enjoy. I'll see you soon."

Danny disconnected the phone on a rush of peace that not only had his sister taken care of a corporate problem, she'd stepped out into the world of dating. Of course he'd be planning a Philly trip soon to check out this Joel. It never hurt a guy to know that a beautiful woman like Mary Clare had a big brother and a father to back her up, although from the sounds of it she was doing quite well on her own, and that felt wonderful.

Now if he could only say the same about himself. He headed into the McGees' store, uncertain what to expect.

"Danny." Kate crossed the floor smiling, a feather duster clutched in her left hand, her movement easier than it had been days ago. "So good to see you. I was just telling Jed that I hope you got our thank-you note."

Danny frowned, confused.

"I sent it to your apartment in Jamison."

That explained the reason he hadn't seen it. Danny hedged. "Life's been crazy busy the past two days, so I'll make sure to check the mail when I get—" He almost said home but stopped himself.

Meg's place wasn't home. His parents' house wasn't home, either, not anymore. Truth be told, he didn't have a place to call home and that didn't feel so good, especially when he'd been contemplating home and hearth the past several weeks.

Kate put a hand on his arm. "Did all this non-sense people are spewing make trouble for you with Meg?"

Danny shrugged, sheepish, not wanting to involve this sweet, old couple.

Kate frowned and worked her jaw before setting the duster down with a thump. "I see it did, and that's just malicious tongues wagging, Danny, a few people who thrive on stirring up trouble. You pay them no mind, you hear?"

He started to reply but she cut him off.

"I mean what I say, and that's one thing you can count on with McGees. We're true to our word, and Jed and I are tickled pink to have an opportunity to rest and relax on our little homestead. There are things we've been putting off for years on account of work and money. You've made that all possible by buying our place here, Danny, and we're grateful."

Her words were so good to hear. He'd been feeling pretty low because Meg thought he'd targeted this benevolent couple, and the fact that Kate was taking his side meant a lot. "Thank you, Kate."

"We'll set things straight, don't you worry." Her voice and manner lent assurance to the simple words. "And that will fix things between you and Meg."

It wouldn't. Danny knew that. If Meg couldn't trust him with a simple thing like buying local real estate, how could she trust him with her heart, her soul, her future? And how could he function knowing she was waiting for him to mess up, to do something underhanded?

Her trust issues had seemed innocent enough, but if a tidbit of idle gossip sent her mind whirling to deception, what kind of life would they have together?

Kate's touch to his arm strengthened. "A few weeks back, the good reverend preached about the Corinthians because the loose talk among them was deceitful, remember?"

Danny nodded, recalling Reverend Hannity's earnest words.

"Those folks saw the truth and the light after a fashion, Danny. Some things might take a little extra time and effort, but they're worth the expenditure."

"You mean Meg."

She nodded. "Yes. And when a girl's been burned twice, she's wise to be more careful in her dealings because while God expects us to help others, He also expects us to protect ourselves with common sense. Meg hasn't had much reason to trust her sensibilities these past couple of years."

Kate made a valid point. Danny had recognized Meg's heightened caution from the beginning.

"Love endures all things," Kate reminded him, the oft-used passage from Corinthians a mainstay in his parents' living room. She faced him, heartfelt. "God's delays are not always denials, young man, they're more like patience builders. Cornerstones. You're young, Danny Romesser. What have you got besides time right now?"

He thought, smiled and dipped his chin in agreement. "Not a thing."

"So do whatever it takes and go get the girl. Wooing and courtship are timeless endeavors, you know."

Whatever it takes…

Danny grinned and gave Kate a big hug. "I'm glad I stopped in here today."

"Me, too. Now go. One of us has some fixing to do and it isn't me."

Danny headed to his car, thoughts formulating in his head. By the time he pulled the car onto Main Street, he'd devised a plan of sorts.

Would it work? Maybe. Maybe not. But Kate was

right, he had time and a clever mind, two precious gifts. Meg had melted into his arms more than once, her feelings obvious. His task was to reignite those feelings and capitalize on the moment. And if that sounded too businesslike, so be it, because this time Danny Romesser meant business.

Chapter Nineteen

Marilyn's eyes grew wide when she entered the kitchen the following morning. "Oh, my dear, what gorgeous flowers. Are they from your beau?"

"No." Oops, Meg didn't mean to sound quite so adamant.

Marilyn offered a wise nod as she slipped into an apron. "I suppose the current term is 'significant other.'"

"Not that either. Just someone I thought I knew."

"Now that sounds ominous." Marilyn headed to the counter, bent and breathed in the bright-toned bouquet, the blended scents permeating the kitchen already. "Oh, lovely. Just lovely. No card?"

"There was." Meg didn't mention that the card was now at the bottom of the wastebasket.

"I see." Marilyn stepped back, smiled and winked. "Playing hard to get is one of those things that either works well or fails miserably, so it's a fine line to walk, but that's all I'm going to say about that. I can see it's not a topic you care to explore this morning."

"Thank you."

"Indeed." Marilyn bobbed her head in quick assent. "I'm moving these out front, though, because this heat is not a bit good for them, delicate and pretty as they are."

She bustled through the Dutch door with the beautiful basket of flowers in hand, intent on her task. Meg opened her mouth to stop her, to say she didn't want or need anyone in the town to see that Danny sent her flowers, but then clamped her lips shut. If she said too much, Marilyn might take up the topic again, and Meg didn't need any more advice for the lovelorn. She'd had her fill, her current circumstance making it impossible to appear in public without seeing whispered asides once again. Ouch.

Marilyn hustled back into the kitchen, her lithe movements belying her years. "I'm so excited to be here, to work with you, get to know you, Meg."

Her enthusiasm softened a hardened edge of Meg's heart. "Me, too. Having you here has been absolutely wonderful."

"Oh, you." Marilyn waved a hand in Meg's direction before bobbing her head toward the front. "Do we have time for the chocolate fudge today?"

"Yes. If you'd like to start the base, I use the same basic recipe for the chocolate, chocolate-almond and chocolate-walnut. I've got pans ready and this recipe is an old favorite."

"It is." Marilyn eyed the card and nodded. "It sets up nice and cuts well. That's so important for presentation, isn't it?"

"Yes, but few people recognize that, Marilyn." Meg eyed her curiously. "Most people just think fudge is fudge."

Marilyn nodded briskly as she gathered ingredients to the right-hand counter. "While I'm not one to go overboard on appearances, gift presentation, well… I wanted those fudge boxes to look just right."

"How sweet." Meg smiled at her, imagining a younger Marilyn with a houseful of kids, making fudge, Christmas lights winking in the background.

"Yes, it was." Marilyn dipped her chin, concentrating on the recipe before her, eyes sharp, each measurement precise, while Meg worked cookie dough in the back corner. Despite the promised sultry summer temperatures, she needed to get cookies baked ahead. Wellsville went over the top with preparations for the rally, and the Russos had been part of the action from the beginning.

As a vendor, Meg rented two hot spots for the weekend. Hannah would run the cookie and coffee booth along the banks of the Genesee River in Island Park, the view of the balloons and the frenetic activity reason enough to get up early and stock the booth predawn on Saturday. The balloon launch's proximity to Danny kept Meg intent on running the Main

Street booth, foregoing the opportunity to see the balloon launches up close and personal. The thought of a face-to-face encounter pushed her pulse into overdrive, making rational thought an irrational concept.

No, she'd nurture the shallow shred of dignity she had left and work the Main Street festival area while Hannah and Crystal staffed the cookie and coffee booth. Maintaining a distance from Danny offered a tiny but tangible strength to her force field. Yeah, he'd scarred its surface with his sweet humor and mind-stopping kisses, but she'd pulled back in time to avoid complete disaster, and that was good.

Except it didn't feel one bit good.

"I plan on helping this weekend too, dear."

Marilyn's spritely voice interrupted Meg's self-harangue. "Marilyn, that might be too much, don't you think? You've been working all week, and it could be really hot on Main Street."

"Don't you worry about me," Marilyn fussed, eyeing the fudge mixture with hawklike intensity. She leaned forward, sniffed, nodded and adjusted the flame downward. "I'm a tough old bird, and I can't wait to be part of the fun. At my age there's precious little left in this world to buy, so shopping the vendors is pointless, whereas helping one—" she beamed a bright smile in Meg's direction "—is a dream come true in so many ways."

"If you're sure…"

"Positive."

The clipped, one-word answer sounded familiar, Danny's quick repartee a thing of the past.

"I'll be here first thing to help load."

What could Meg say? She needed the help. Her parents would be there off and on, but they were big rally supporters with their own volunteer commitments throughout the day. "Thank you, Marilyn."

The older woman's smile blossomed like a brown-eyed Susan beneath a full sun. "You're quite welcome, dear."

"We're loaded?"

"Done." Meg's father headed toward the driver's side early Saturday morning. "I'll drop Hannah's inventory off first, then circle up to your stand once the send-off crowd thins."

"Great. Thanks, Dad."

"No problem. And your mother will be along later with Ben."

Meg nodded as she headed for her car. "It's not like her to miss a morning launch. You're sure she's okay?"

"She's fine, just a little behind because of all the work she's been doing. And she's picking up Ben, so that's a difference this year."

"Good point. Driving to his place and then all the way back up here would have been silly."

"Exactly what she thought, so she'll see you later. It will take me a little while to get through to Hannah, so don't hurry down to your booth."

"Gotcha." The Main Street Festival followed the early morning balloon launch, giving the Main Street vendors more time to get ready. "Marilyn and I will see you later, then."

He nodded, tipped his scarred baseball cap Marilyn's way and eased the van onto the road.

"Meg?"

Meg turned, sucked in a deep breath and refused to contemplate what could go wrong this day if she and Danny crossed paths. Surely he'd have the good sense not to browse the festival site, wouldn't he?

Marilyn took a plain, brown paper bag out of her satchel and handed it to Meg. "I made this for you, dear. I hope you don't mind or think it's presumptuous, but I know you've missed dressing your part this week and this might help."

"What on Earth?"

The older woman sent her a quick, endearing smile. "Just a little gift from an old lady who loves to work with calico."

"Calico?" Meg opened the bag and sighed. "Oh, Marilyn, how did you know?"

"About the material?" Marilyn smiled her delight. "You like it, don't you? I wondered if it would suit you, but Maude said you and your young man were in the shop not too long ago and you expressed a preference for the tea-stained blue calico, so I thought—" she shrugged and waved a hand toward the candy store and Meg "—that this would be a nice thank-you for letting me work here, letting me be part of the fun."

"Marilyn..." Meg didn't know what to say. Quick tears pricked her eyes, the aged woman's thoughtfulness a blessing beyond measure. "I—"

"And look here." Marilyn's voice washed away the tears. "I made this sleeve open to ease over your cast, that way you can wear this now. Once you've healed, I'll just nip a seam in there quick as a wink and it's good as new."

Warmth crept into the rocky place Meg had called a heart the past week. Sweet warmth, like a fresh-glazed cookie, melt-in-your-mouth good. She reached out and grabbed Marilyn into a hug. "Thank you."

Marilyn returned the hug then tapped her watch. "But we'd best get a move on if we're to see the launch, hadn't we, dear?"

The launch. Of course Marilyn would want to see the launch, and even though it was the last thing Meg wanted to see, she nodded graciously. "Of course. Let me slip into this and we'll be off."

"Do you need assistance?"

Meg smiled and held up the open sleeve. "Not with this."

"Then I'll be in the car."

Early morning fog shrouded the Genesee River valley. The launch would be delayed until the fog cleared. Visibility was huge in ballooning, and some mornings presented a challenge.

Marilyn peered through the windshield, her excitement palpable. "This brings back so many memories."

"Of?"

Marilyn furrowed her brow, tightened her jaw and shrugged as if upset that she'd spoken out loud.

"Do you like balloon launches, Marilyn?"

"I like festivals." She angled her head, the warm brown eyes peppered with golden sparks, well-used laugh lines crinkling Meg's way. "They're vibrant. Alive with characters."

Meg wouldn't disagree there. Every festival had its fill of characters, and Wellsville was no different. She pulled down the back road, parked the car in the vendor lot and headed up a decorated alley with Marilyn. She paused at the roadside, frowned, turned then frowned again. "We're supposed to be right there." Meg pointed to a fried dough stand. "That's been my spot for years."

Marilyn headed across the street at a quick clip. "Let's see what's up, hmm?"

Meg hurried after her, the fog shadowing shapes of curbside tables and booths, giving Main Street an eerie effect in the thin light.

"The committee called me with the change Thursday night," the gal setting up the fried dough booth explained. "I got home from shopping for the festival and had the message waiting."

"But I never heard a thing," Meg countered. "And my dad will have no idea—"

"Meg? That you?" Her father's voice hailed her through the morning dampness. "We're down here."

Meg offered a quick thanks to the fried dough vendor and headed south on Main Street. As she neared the site of her booth, her feet paused. "No."

"What dear?" Marilyn pressed forward, peering. "What's wrong?"

"They put us in front of Jed and Kate McGee's store."

"We don't like them?"

Meg shook her head, confused and dismayed. "Oh, we like them just fine, we love them, they're great, but…"

"But?"

"They just sold their store to a man who's going to put a candy store there. A Grandma Mary's candy store."

"And that makes you angry." Marilyn nodded as if that was the most sensible thing she'd ever heard.

"No, not at all," Meg assured her. "He's opening it for his grandmother, and I think that's wonderful— although it's a little scary for me from a business perspective, but I'm not afraid of a little competition." Meg eyed the store, then shrugged. "Well, a lot of competition, actually."

"Well, then, I'm confused. Why don't we want to be here, in front of this store?"

"Because what if he comes by? I can't see him now. That would be horrible."

Marilyn flexed her brow as she attempted to sort through Meg's ramblings, then gave up visibly. "I'm lost, dear."

"I thought I loved him."

"Ah." Marilyn's face softened measurably. "Now we're getting somewhere. And he loved you?"

Meg shook her head. "I thought so, but when I heard how he pushed these old people out of their store, I went a little crazy on him."

Marilyn patted her arm much like one would soothe an irate child. "It's a woman's prerogative, dear."

"I kicked him out."

"He was living with you?"

"No, of course not, but I rented him the apartment next door because if I didn't Brad and Denise would have wanted it, and the last thing I needed was my former fiancé—"

"One of them," Marilyn interjected. She raised one shoulder in response to Meg's questioning look. "Maude filled me in."

Of course she did.

"I had no choice but to rent the apartment to him, and he turned out to be so nice and helpful, funny and sweet, so kind…" Meg thought of how respectfully Danny handled Ben, of his affability with her parents, his ease at blending into any situation, how wonderful it had felt to be part of that and how crushed she'd been to realize it was all an act.

"Meg, you want these here?" Her father interrupted their conversation by hoisting a waxed box of fudge into the air.

"No, I want them there." Meg scowled and pointed to her allocated spot a block and a half north. "But obviously that's not going to happen."

"I'll stack them here and you can decide where each variety goes when you're done talking."

"Venting, actually," Marilyn called after him. She turned back to Meg, eyes wide with understanding. "So you chucked him, did you?"

"Yes."

"I did that once." Marilyn moved behind the booth and started organizing the fudge trays according to the stickers along the clear acrylic front panel. "By the time I realized my mistake, I had my share of groveling to do, but Gerald had a forgiving heart. And he liked my fudge. A lot."

"Really?"

The old woman's gaze softened with aged wisdom. She nodded. "Oh, yes. Sometimes a woman is so sure she's right when she's the most wrong." She swept the street a quick glance of appraisal, then nodded Meg's way. "The fog is lifting."

"It is."

Sunlight dappled the shadows, points of brightness tweaking the fog, shifting it, moving it, drying it. As the sun burst through, the vendors moved into the street as one, eyes skyward, watching and waiting.

One by one, balloons dotted the air, rising from

behind the trees of Island Park, their launch a kaleidoscope of quiet gentility, the deep blue July sky a perfect backdrop.

Danny was up there. Meg knew it, knew to look for a spectral balloon, the "Chasing Rainbows" theme indicative of Danny's colors. Several rainbow-toned balloons danced through the air, and Meg scoured the baskets, wondering if she'd see him, if she could make him out before his balloon got too high.

Marilyn gripped her arm. "Oh, honey, look at that one!"

Meg tilted her head, disbelief making her heart skip a beat while warmth pooled low in her belly as a beautiful ascending rainbow balloon waved a banner that read: "Megs, will you marry me? Chase rainbows with me?"

Her father appeared at her side, his grin saying he'd known all along. "You need a ride to the put-down site, Meg?"

"I can cover things here," Marilyn assured her. "If sixty years in the candy business doesn't equip me for running a festival fudge booth, then I've been tap-dancing my way through life."

"Sixty years?" Meg didn't know which way to turn first. Her eyes were glued to the banner, but once Marilyn's words registered, she swung around. "Are you—?"

"Danny's grandmother, Grandma Mary, at your service. And you, young lady—" she gave Meg a little shove toward her father "—have a drop site to get to. I think my grandson is showing *güt gut* by proclaiming his love for you in front of the whole community. You don't want to keep him waiting, do you?" She reached forward and cradled Meg's cheeks in her hands, her smile an entreaty. "I think you've both waited long enough to find one another, and if I want to have a hand in raising my great-grandchildren, we need to get this show on the road."

Her father tooted the horn as things started to make perfect sense to Meg. Marilyn's affinity to the kitchen, her husband, Gerald...Danny had told her about Uncle Jerry, no doubt named for his father, Gerald.

Bits and pieces slipped into place. Obviously her booth had been shifted south to allow her a view of the launch and Danny's banner. She should probably be mad that he'd taken so many liberties, but how could she be upset when her dreams called to her from overhead? "Is that Ben up there with him?"

"It is." Her father grinned at her from the driver's seat. "Ben was understandably excited to go up, although your mother read him a prelaunch riot act. Danny said his uncle Jerry would never go up in the balloon, but that he'd crew from below, always on the pickup truck, ready to help."

"Quite true." Marilyn's eyes misted at the memory. She waved her hand upward. Danny and Ben waved back, their features indistinct, but Ben's excitement was obvious even from this far away.

Meg scooted in alongside her father, her heart bursting, the ache in her chest replaced by sheer anticipation. "Can you get through the traffic?"

Her father clapped the magnetic Vendor sign to the roof. "Vendors and ambulances get priority treatment this weekend, honey."

Meg laughed. Of course they did, and well they should. It was the Great Wellsville Balloon Rally, after all, and she knew great things were about to happen.

And about time, too.

She hadn't come.

Danny scanned the perimeters of the hay lot as *Chasing Rainbows* lost altitude, but other than a smattering of cars and his pickup truck and trailer, they were quite alone, no Russos in sight to welcome them back to the ground.

He worked to hide his disappointment from Ben and the crewman, but his heart settled like lead weight in his chest. He'd listened to Grandma and Kate McGee, he'd sent flowers and notes and had publicly proposed, but obviously the lady wasn't interested.

Not interested? Are you forgetting the way her hand fit in yours like they melded as one? Who are you kidding?

"Boss, you want this banner folded?" the crewman asked.

Burned might be a better choice. Danny eyed the crumpled banner and shrugged. "It's not like I can use it again."

"Well, you could, I suppose."

Somewhere in the midst of those five little words his heart resuscitated. He turned, tugged by the sheer pleasure of hearing her voice, knowing she was there, that she came to meet him. "To what end, Megs?"

She smiled up at him, joy brightening her eyes, her cheeks, her gaze, an old-fashioned calico dress making her look too good to be true. "Well if I say no, you could just change the name."

"What if I don't want to change the name, Megs?" He moved closer until only a breath of air separated them, a thin breath at that. "What if there's only one woman who can ever make me happy? Be my bride, my wife? Have my babies?"

"Then she'd be a fool to say no, Danny, and despite my track record, I'm no fool."

He grinned and grazed her lips a kiss, soft and gentle. "Is that a yes?"

"Most assuredly. And can we make this soon, please? Your grandmother has informed me that she's moving back here to help raise her great-grandchildren."

"Oh, she did, did she?" Danny eased back, smiling, his hands cradling her cheeks, her face, her hair. "And as you've discovered, I hate to disappoint Grandma."

"Understandable, because she's a doll. I can see where you got your charm." She leaned back, braced by his hold, his touch. "Yes, I'll marry you, Danny Romesser. And I'll have your babies. And I might even ride in your balloon."

He took her mouth in a sweet kiss of betrothal that was almost instantly interrupted by cheering. Danny looked up, bemused. "Where did all these people come from?"

Megan glanced around and grinned. "A logical guess would be the balloon rally. When you propose in front of thousands of people, you're likely to gather an audience. Once they can get through the traffic, that is."

Danny laughed out loud. "Well, since you said yes, I don't care who knows. How soon can we get a license, Megs?"

"We'll get it once my busy season is past and your store is successfully opened," she told him. "Business first, Danny."

Grinning, he swept her off her feet in a big hug, swinging her around to the delight of the crowd. "I can promise you, Megs, that from this day forward it will never be business first again."

She planted a kiss to his lips, her promise and pledge. "You've got that right, Danny-boy."

Epilogue

"A perfect day for a wedding, Meg." Karen adjusted Meg's veil, stepped back and smiled her approval.

"And then some." Meg's dad stepped into the room and handed her a note. "Danny asked me to deliver this."

"Did you read it first?" Meg asked, teasing. "Because I've been dumped via phone and text in the past. A note would just add insult to injury."

Adam chucked her under the chin. "Read the note and see."

Meg opened the envelope, scanned the contents, smiled and walked to the open window. Early fall colors backlit the town park in ribbons of green, gold and crimson, while mums blanketed the churchyard in a perfumed hue of country shades against dark green grass. "Hey, you."

"Hey, you." Danny grinned up from below. He put a finger to his lips then splayed his hands wide while keeping his voice soft. "Just wanted you to know I was here, Megs, and properly dressed for the occasion."

She leaned out the window, wondering how she could have ever thought Brad or Michael would be The One, grateful she hadn't made such a serious mistake and certain that Danny in a tux was a God-given gift to womankind. "I didn't doubt it for a minute, Danny."

Her words broadened his smile. "Really?"

"Really, truly."

"I love you, Megs."

She blushed, heat invading her cheeks, excitement warming her from within despite the cool, fall breeze. "I love you, too."

Marilyn approached from the side church steps. She slipped an arm around Danny's waist. He dropped a kiss to his grandmother's cheek and raised his gaze once more. "And you're sure you won't mind being part of the biggest candy conglomerate on the East Coast?"

"The concept is growing on me." Megs grinned from her lofty parapet and blew them a kiss. "And since I changed my official business name to the Colonial *Cookie* Kitchen as of last Saturday, you won't have to worry about my little store putting Grandma Mary's out of business."

Marilyn sent her a quick smile of approval. "I'm breathing easier just knowing that, honey."

Meg laughed and followed Marilyn's progress as she headed back into the church. "She's wonderful."

"She says the same about you. You ready to make this official, Megs?" He jerked a thumb toward the church sanctuary.

"Ready when you are."

He stepped back, blew her a kiss and blessed her with a smile that said he was more than ready for everything awaiting them. "I'll meet you inside."

"Sounds good."

The trill of sweet music called the attendants. Alyssa and Hannah took their spots, with Alyssa's little girl, Cory, leading the way, a basket of flowers clutched tight in her four-year-old hands. Her baby brother, Clay, sat in a front pew with her daddy and big brother.

Meg smiled at her parents. "This time you actually get to walk me down the aisle. But I promise you one thing." She leaned up and pressed a kiss to both their cheeks. "You will never have to do this again."

"Music to my ears, Meg."

"I'm just happy I finally get to wear this dress." Karen smoothed a hand over the gauzy, gold fabric, hints of beaded sparkle kicking back light. "Although I was more than happy to buy you a new one, dear."

Meg checked her reflection in the mirror one last

time, the simple A-line strapless dress gracious and gorgeous all at once. "And I love that Marilyn made my veil. And that she's moving down here for her retirement."

Adam proffered his arm. "She loves being back in town, meeting her old friends."

"That's what she told you, Dad?"

"She did."

"And you bought that?"

Adam frowned. "Of course. Why else would she move down here?"

Karen sent him a look that said more than words. "She wants to babysit her great-grandchildren, dear. When they come."

Adam laughed and hugged Meg's shoulders. "Well, I can't deny I'm looking forward to being a grandpa after so many false starts." He saw the look Meg shot him and pulled back. "But first, the wedding."

"That would be nice. Are we ready? And can I trust both of you to behave yourselves? No jokes at the bride's expense?"

"None."

"Promise."

She grasped their arms as they moved forward, the sweet sounds of fairy music Meg's cue to appear on the white satin runner. She stepped through the oak-trimmed entry and caught sight of Danny at the front of the church. He winked and smiled, one brow raised in appreciation for the dress and the woman wearing it.

And that was a feeling Meg would have a lifetime to enjoy.

* * * * *

*Look for the next book
in the Men of Allegany County series,
MENDED HEARTS,
coming soon
only from Love Inspired.*

Meg's Allegany Maple Fudge

- 2 cups packed dark brown sugar
- ¾ cup evaporated milk
- ⅓ cup *real* maple syrup (Meg prefers "dark amber" for richer flavor)
- 1 cup butter (do not, repeat, do not use margarine. Really. Truly.)
- 2 cups powdered sugar
- 1 cup walnuts or pecans
- ½ teaspoon vanilla

Butter a 9"x13" pan, then line the pan with heavy-duty aluminum foil for ease in cutting.

Combine sugar, butter, milk and maple syrup in a medium saucepan. Bring to boil over medium heat. Reduce heat slightly and boil for 10 minutes, stirring constantly. Overcooking toughens the consistency of the fudge, so watch the clock or set a timer, and don't think you can walk away and do laundry or answer the phone, because my experience tells me that tiny duties inevitably stretch into elongated ones and so I often burn the first batch.

You'd think I'd learn after a while, wouldn't you?

Remove from heat, add powdered sugar and vanilla. A teaspoon of maple flavoring may be added at this time, but isn't really necessary. Beat by hand (this is a preemptive strike against high calorie intake, because this fudge is irresistible and any exercise you can get ahead of time keeps you ahead of the game) or with hand mixer until thick and glossy. Mix in walnuts and pour into prepared pan. Refrigerate until set.

To cut: Slide foil out of greased pan, place on countertop or suitable cutting board and use sharp, thin-bladed knife or fudge/brownie cutter.

Store in airtight container.

This fudge freezes well, keeps in refrigerator well.

Dear Reader,

We raised our six kids in a sweet, small town. We understand the good and bad of that. Small towns embrace their own, have an enduring ambiance and there's nothing like Friday night football under the lights. The downside is that everyone dies famous; there are few secrets and little discretion at times.

We encouraged our children to grow wings, but like any gardener, I wanted to show the importance of a good root system. It's easy to forget the legacy, work, traditions and the backbone once you're ingrained in another time and another place, but those original roots help keep us anchored, nurtured and focused. In *Small-Town Hearts,* Danny finds comfort for youthful indiscretions in an old faith renewed, an old town refurbished and his grandmother's truisms that linger at every turn. And he finds his match when he meets his competition, our spunky Meg, an Old World-style entrepreneur who's been burned because she's anxious to hurry God's plan, force His hand.

I love this story of "third time's a charm." Let me know what you think by visiting the "guys" and me at www.menofalleganycounty.com or drop by "Ruthy's Place" at www.ruthysplace.com. You can also reach me by emailing me at ruthy@ruthlogan-herne.com or snail mail me c/o Love Inspired Books,

233 Broadway, Suite 1001, New York, NY 10279.
I look forward to hearing from you and swapping
stories and recipes!

In His hands, in His time,

Ruthy

QUESTIONS FOR DISCUSSION

1. Danny expects to while away his summer in a sleepy small town, champing at the bit to get back to his big-city East Coast venue. When he falls in love with the sweet ambiance of Allegany County and realizes that making a living in a small town is no simple matter, he gets a first-hand education he hadn't expected. How often do we make assumptions about people, places or things only to discover the truth is quite different?

2. God has blessed Meg with patience, focus and talent in the business world, but she can't seem to bring those gifts into her love life because she's guilty of rushing the process. Are we so anxious to find the dream that we sometimes forget to enjoy the journey?

3. Danny has a great relationship with his parents and grandmother, but his one major regret is not spending time with his developmentally disabled uncle before Uncle Jerry's death. Instead of seeing the selfishness of youth as a temporary aberration, Danny sees himself as selfish and self-absorbed. Meeting Ben becomes his chance to set things right personally and emotionally. Has God ever provided you with those second

chances, those "coincidences" that help move you forward?

4. Meg's parents are facing a big decision with Ben. The thought of pushing a developmentally challenged child out the nest weighs heavily on them. How difficult is it to push people into new challenges when you really, truly long to protect them from all harm?

5. Meg's a born romantic with an eye on her biological clock. As years tick on and the dream eludes us, what role does faith play in our personal quests?

6. Danny uses quiet strength and humor as a defuser throughout this story. How does humor help you to keep things in their proper perspective?

7. Meg is happy to be a hometown girl despite the downside of being talked about chronically in the public eye. She stayed close for college and built her business right in her hometown. What does that tell us about her? Is it good or bad to cling fiercely to one's roots?

8. Danny hides who he is initially, but as his feelings grow, he confesses about his job. Should he have come clean sooner?

9. Danny's sympathy for his sister's loss prods him to rethink his mother's corporate decisions. His nurturing side wants to help Mary Clare, but he recognizes her need to spread her wings. How hard is it to sit back and watch loved ones mature through sometime painful experiences?

10. Danny's growing relationship with Ben is the second chance he's been looking for. What does his respect for Ben as a person tell us about Danny?

11. The Holy Spirit offers blessings and wisdom in numerous ways, some subtle, some not. Why do we tend to resist until the last possible chance?

12. Grandma Mary bustles into town like a tiny hurricane, her zest and zeal the benchmark for what built the family candy company. She keeps her identity from Meg because she knows Meg needs help and support. Could this lie of omission have backfired?

13. Danny comes to town on a simple mission but ends up with a crash course in faith, romance, small business administration and small-town dynamics. He definitely got more than he bargained for. Think about times when little tasks or jobs in your life have led to much more momentous occasions. Isn't it amazing how our path unwinds before us?

LARGER-PRINT BOOKS!

**GET 2 FREE
LARGER-PRINT NOVELS
PLUS 2 FREE
MYSTERY GIFTS**

Love Inspired®

Larger-print novels are now available...

LILPI I

SUSPENSE

RIVETING INSPIRATIONAL ROMANCE

Watch for our series of edge-
of-your-seat suspense novels.
These contemporary tales
of intrigue and romance
feature Christian characters
facing challenges to their faith...
and their lives!

**AVAILABLE IN REGULAR
& LARGER-PRINT FORMATS**

For exciting stories that reflect traditional values,
visit:
www.ReaderService.com